JUST ONE *Touch*

Author of the Kiss Me Crazy Series

JAMI ROGERS

To my family.
Thank you for always being there and loving me.
I love you, too.

Just One Touch

Copyright © 2016 by Jami Rogers

All rights reserved.

No part of this book may be reproduced or transmitted in any form or by any means, electronic or mechanical, including photocopying, recording, or by any information storage and retrieval system without the written permission of the author, except for the use of brief quotations in a review.

This is a work of fiction. Names, characters, businesses, places, events and incidents are either the products of the author's imagination or used in a fictitious manner. Any resemblance to actual persons, living or dead, or actual events is purely coincidental.

Editor: Julie Sturgeon, CEOEditor, ceoeditor.com

Copyediting/Proofreading: Casey Dawes, Concierge Self-Publishing, www.ConciergeSelfPublishing.com

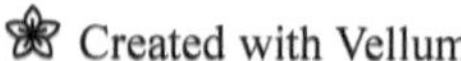 Created with Vellum

JUST ONE *Touch*

Author of the Kiss Me Crazy Series

JAMI ROGERS

JUST ONE TOUCH

THE BLACK ALCOVE SERIES BOOK 3

JAMI ROGERS

CHAPTER ONE

Conner

I can and I will be a great father for my son.

"Dad! Dad! Did you see?" Jake stands in front of me, his arms swinging as he catches his breath. "I almost made it. Uncle E didn't lift me high enough."

I shoot a look toward Ethan that says *next time you make sure my kid makes the basket*, but he and our good friend Logan are too busy playing one-on-one at this point.

"Next time, bud, I bet you make it."

"I hope so! I wanna be the best like you, Dad."

I grin as he takes a juice pouch from the cooler near the driveway and sits on the grass next to me, his legs bent and arms resting by the elbows over his kneecaps, just like me.

I wanna be the best like you, Dad.

His words strike me right in the chest. I don't ever want him to think otherwise. He doesn't know that every night he isn't with me, I'm working shifts to make enough money to pay my rent because I want him to have a warm place to come home to when I have custody. I moved out of my sister's basement and into my own apartment four months ago. Rent isn't cheap.

"Where did Aunt Kelsey go?" he asks, twisting on his bum to find her. His hand holding the Capri Sun squeezes a little too tight, causing fruit punch to squirt out of the straw. The liquid lands on his cream plaid shorts. Thank God it's clear liquid and not red. Stains in clothes are not an area of my expertise. The wet spot blends right in with the dirt and grass stains he got earlier playing with his two-year-old cousin and my niece Clara, Kelsey and Ethan's daughter.

He notices the new spill and attempts to brush it off, only soaking it in more.

"She went inside to get a surprise for you. Why don't you go get Uncle E and Logan and tell them to come sit until Kelsey comes back outside?"

"Okay!" His entire face beams with excitement. His juice packet is thrown to the side as he takes off running across the driveway. I notice his untied shoelace a step too late. He hits the concrete, skidding his knee across the hard surface. I'm off the grass before he can get up. In a swift move I pick him up at the waist, place him back on his feet, and kneel in front of him. Logan and Ethan come up behind me.

"Hey, bud, what happened?" Logan asks.

"That was quiet the digger you took," Ethan says.

Jake looks between them and back to me. I can see the tears trying to fight their way out, but he's fighting harder not to cry in front of anyone right now. I stubbed my pinky toe the other day when we were at home. Jake asked why I didn't cry, and I told him it was because I'm a man and men don't cry.

He then told me he was a man, too. My heart swells and I feel like a damn sap.

He wants to be just like me.

"That's going to make a nice battle wound." Logan points to Jake's new bloody knee. "Does it hurt?"

Jake looks at me quickly before he shrugs his little shoulders. "No, I'll be fine," he says before squirming out of my hold. He starts to walk away from the circle we've made toward the side garage door. Probably to go inside where my sister is.

"How about we get it cleaned up?" I suggest. I'm sure he hasn't thought of that, but he'll pretend he has and act like he doesn't need me. A phase I hope he grows out of, soon.

"I can do it," he says without stopping and quickly is inside the house.

"You've got a tough guy on your hands these days, huh?" Logan asks, chuckling as the basketball shoots from his hands, hitting nothing but net.

"He better be tough. I'm going to need someone to look after Clara when she starts going to school," Ethan adds as he swoops up the ball from under the hoop.

"Yeah, that's a few years away, and that's only if Heather agrees to let him go to school in Wind Valley. She has till the end of the summer to decide, and I suggested making a decision sooner to help with getting the paperwork done, but that's only made things worse."

"Why would she even consider him attending school in Envy? It's a small town with a school of like ten kids. If Jake went to Wind Valley, he'd have way more options in everything: sports, clubs, and academics. Plus, WV is only a twenty-minute drive from Envy. She should suck it up for Jake."

Leave it to Logan to be all about the facts. I swear, since he found out his wife, Sara, was expecting, this whole new person came out of him.

"If she picks Envy, it's only because of my lack of trying."

"Trying to what?" Logan asks.

I scratch the back of my neck as I look away. How can I explain to them that Heather has suggested dating, without getting the dead-stare look they always give me? The one that says, *I wish I could help, but I have no idea what to say right now.* "She wants to give the family thing a try," I say, summing it up quick.

Single me is screaming no every time I think about it. Father me—he doesn't want to rule out anything that could be the best decision for my son.

And, yep, right there, that's the look. The basketball stays pinned under Ethan's arms as they stare at me.

"Like, as a couple and not just Jake's parents?" Ethan asks.

"You and Heather?" Logan asks at the same time.

"Yep," I answer, nodding slowly. "That's her idea."

"The same woman who made all these crazy rules for you to follow so you could get time alone with Jake. The crazy mother who didn't want you around and wouldn't agree with anything you said?" I don't miss Logan's concern buried in the tone of his voice.

"Yeah, that's about my exact thought process," I tell him. After all, for the first two years of Jake's life, she didn't tell me I had a son. *You're irresponsible and can't even take care of yourself. There was no way I was going to put my child in your hands.*

"When did she decide this?" Ethan asks.

"About two days ago."

"Well, crap, what are you going to do?"

I shrug, because that's my only reaction to the entire idea. I still can't wrap my head around the fact she even came up with it. We were never a couple to begin with. We fooled around once, that was it. Why try now? And it's not that she isn't attractive, I just don't feel a connection with her other than Jake. I've seen the way my friends are with their wives or the way they talk about them when they aren't. I don't have that for Heather.

"I don't want to say I'm 100 percent against the idea, but forcing feelings for someone and then it not working out doesn't sound like anything that ends well."

"Do you think you could have feelings for Heather?" Logan asks.

"Maybe. I mean, we fooled around one night and now this is where we end up. I haven't really made much of an effort to get to know her outside of who is doing what for Jake."

"So you think if you get to know her, you might develop real feelings for her?" Ethan asks this time.

"There's only one way to find out, right? If it means giving Jake a good life, I should try anything."

"Well, I guess there's your answer," Logan says.

"Yeah, I suppose you're right."

"And you know, if you need to talk or maybe get a woman's perspective without leading Heather on, Kelsey might be able to help," Ethan adds.

I nod—my sister would be the right person to talk to about

this—but Heather is really who I should go to. Communication is what will make this work the best.

I pull my cell from my pocket to shoot her a text asking if we can meet for ice cream before my shift at the BA tonight.

The garage door opens and Clara steps out in a blue and white polka dot dress, her brown hair looking a bit ratty from a day of playing with her cousin. Her steps are slow as she focuses on the paper bowl in her hands with a scoop of ice cream in it. Jake comes out next, his steps just as cautious for the same reason and a bandage over his knee. Then Kelsey pokes her head out, holding the door open enough to show a glimpse of her seven months' baby bump.

"I have a bowl for each of you, if you want to come get it."

You don't have to tell us twice.

Once we've all settled down in the grass and eaten our ice cream, I glance at my watch. I told Heather we could meet in an hour.

"Jake, why don't you head on over to Grandma and Grandpa's and give them a hug goodbye?" With them living across the street from my sister, it's easier to visit everyone when we come here.

"Do I have to leave?" His tiny, sad voice breaks my heart.

"Yeah, bud, your mom misses you the way I do when you're gone." I ruffle his head and mess up the same chocolate-brown hair that I have in the process.

I can't read the blank expression on his face, but based on his resistance to move right now, I don't want to know what he's thinking.

My little man stops at the sidewalk and looks both ways before he crosses the street. At four years old, he should be by my side for this journey, but with it being a slow neighborhood, the group of us observing from the grass and my parents, standing on their porch, I think he's just fine crossing on his own.

He gives them each a hug and then repeats his process back across the street. A few more hugs later, we're in my truck and headed back to my apartment. I only glance in the rearview mirror a few times, because the bummed out look on his face is heartbreaking. I don't want him to go either, and if I could say anything to him without tearing up myself, I'd want him to know that I'm fighting for him. To be a part of his life, to make sure he is always taken care of.

Being a family could give me all that.

I pull up in front of my apartment building. It's a fourplex, and looks just like the two buildings on each side of it. All of them could use a coat of fresh green paint and landscaping wouldn't hurt either. The bedrooms are a little small and the kitchens could definitely use an upgrade, but the rent is reasonable and it's walking distance from my job at the Black Alcove Bar.

I put the gear of my red, four-door Ford truck into park and take notice of the moving truck out front and the small, white Corolla that's in my usual parking spot. There is a heart sticker in the window with the number 26.2 in the center. That can only mean one thing. The new tenant, the one moving in across the hall from me, is crazy and a runner. All runners are crazy in my opinion. What a boring sport.

"Hey, bud, let's keep the secret of you having ice cream at

Aunt Kelsey's house between us, okay?" I say, catching his attention in the rearview mirror. Heather would not be too impressed if she knew he ate ice cream twice in one day when he's staying at her place tonight. Bedtime will be fun for her.

My bad.

"Why?" he asks.

"If we keep it a 'Daddy and me' secret, maybe we can do it again someday," I reply instantly, because I knew that he would ask why. His eyes light up and he nods numerous times.

With a shake of my head, I turn off the engine and hop out, opening Jake's door just in time for him to jump out, too. He thinks he's cool because he can unhook his seat belt and doesn't need his dad to do it, but one time he did it too soon was all it took for him to learn it's even cooler to wait until the truck is turned off before he pulls on the buckle.

He doesn't say anything, but he peeks inside the white truck, taking note of the fact that only a few boxes and a chair are left to move.

"That looks like our chair, Dad." Jake points right before he starts to climb in, but I tug him back by his back belt loop.

"That's not our stuff, bud. Let's go inside, alright? I'm just going to grab the mail and I'll meet you in there. Wait for me once you're inside."

He nods fast, walking straight for the doors like I taught him. *Don't stop for anyone.*

I watch him the entire time until his little body is completely inside. The mail contains just another power bill and an issue of *American Motorcyclist*. I tuck both pieces under my arm as I open the door. I expect to find Jake standing in front of our apartment door, quietly waiting for me, because that's our agreement during this phase, but he isn't. He's standing in front of the door across the hall, talking to our new neighbor instead.

"Yeah, and then my Uncle E"—deep breath—"he picked me up and I didn't make it." He takes another deep breath as he finishes giving what I'm guessing is the quickest rundown of his afternoon.

My mouth is half open, ready to start in on my "what did I tell you about talking to strangers?" talk when I take the last step inside the building, allowing his chatter companion to come into view.

Long and tan legs, toned from what I'm going to assume is a crap load of running, stand before me in a pair of cut-off jean shorts and a black Nirvana t-shirt that hugs a perfect rack. Blond hair is pulled up into a messy, sexy-as-hell bun on top of her head with a few wisps of hair falling down her face. Crystal clear eyes like diamonds with just a hint of blue in the center catch my gaze, and I'm completely drawn to them. When she smiles, any lecture I'm about to give is fully forgotten.

"Hi, I'm Alex." Her eyes are trained on me as her grin stays put.

"Conner," I reply, grinning back, and that's when I realize there is a dresser, a mattress, and multiple boxes blocking our apartment door. This isn't a very big entryway. I don't even know how they got all this in here. I check my watch again.

"Are they going to be much longer to move this?" I ask, pointing to all the stuff in front of my door.

"Dad, is she our new neighbor?" Jake tugs on my hand.

"No," she says, peering out the front door behind me. "They said they were taking a quick break, though."

"A quick break? I have somewhere I need to be." Heather likes promptness. Showing up late isn't in the plans for me.

"Oh," is all she says, followed by a forced frown and shrug. "Maybe you could get inside through a window?"

"A window?" She can't be serious. Her response tells me she doesn't care about the inconvenience she's causing me. "You think I should take my son and break into my own apartment through a window?

"Or you just cool down and wait. It was just a suggestion." Her stance changes as her hip pops to the left and she crosses her arms.

My left brow cocks at the fact that she actually seems irritated by *me*. I'll just take care of it myself. I may be overreacting, but if her attitude right now is any indication of what kind of uncaring neighbor is moving in across the hall from me, I'm not thrilled, and the less interaction we have, the better.

I grab a box and turn for her apartment. She cuts me off before I make it through the doorway, and I have to take a deep breath before I lose that so called "cool" she thinks I need to find. I need in inside my apartment if we're going to meet Heather on time, and I refuse to wait for her or her worthless movers to move all of this junk. Whether she likes it or not, I'm doing it myself.

Alexis

"What do you think you're doing?" I ask, pulling my view from the bulging biceps that are tugging against his shirt as he holds one of my boxes in front of him. Typical guy, taking charge of the situation, like a girl doesn't have the aggression to do it herself.

"I don't have time to wait on your lazy movers," he says, nudging me with the box to move out of his way.

"Put my things down." I push back against the cardboard. This guy can't just walk in here and tell people what to do or be rude for no reason. It wasn't like I told my movers to put my stuff in front of his door so I could have a rocky start with a new neighbor. Being in this town has my nerves on edge enough as it is.

"Just let me move your shit," he says.

"Dad, you said a bad word!"

"Jake, sit on the steps while Dad helps move this lady's things, okay?"

Great, I have a neighbor who thinks he owns the place and can do whatever he wants with my stuff.

"That won't be necessary because you aren't touching any of my shit," I say, and immediately cringe that I just swore in front of his little boy.

Conner, I think he said his name is, rolls his eyes and then nudges me again. This time I try to yank the box out of his grip. He doesn't let go, so I do it again.

"Fine," he growls at the same time I give up, thinking he isn't giving up, but I am wrong. The box drops, shattering the moment it meets the floor. Oh my god, I'm going to kill him. He had better hope that wasn't valuable. I kneel to the floor, flipping one tab of the box open, and my eyes find the broken frame. Tears fall immediately. The clay frame my brother made me before we were split into two different fosters homes is broken into pieces.

"Look, I didn't—"

"You should have just listened to me!" I stand and push the box into my apartment with my foot.

"I was just trying to help you," he argues.

"I didn't ask for your help!" I yell again as more tears come. I turn, prepared to slam my door in his face and hopefully hit him with it in the process when two small eyes grab my attention. His son is staring right at me, blinking and looking ready to cry as well. I sniffle and take a deep breath before I calmly close my door.

I let out a couple more slow breaths and slide down the door, sitting next to the box. I pull out the pieces of the frame, running my fingers over the sharp edges of the blue, green, and yellow pieces. Next I pull out the faded photo that used to being inside it and choke back more tears when I notice a corner stuck to part of the frame, leaving it ripped.

My last memory of my brother, Logan, is of when we were making these picture frames in the children's home, before they separated us. It was like he knew they couldn't keep us together. He was hugging me, telling me to be brave, that I was the strongest little girl he knew, and that no matter what, I'd see him again one day. For some reason, this frame and the fact I kept it in good condition gave me hope that his words were true.

Now it's broken and I hope I never run into my jackhole of a neighbor ever again. Coming to Wind Valley has been the worst decision I've ever made.

* * *

Between my afternoon moving in and plotting how, if, or when I tell my brother I'm here, my stress level was starting to get out of hand. Yoga has always been my go-to when I'm overwhelmed, and since I'd applied for a job at this gym before I moved here, I knew they offered classes. This class, however, wasn't what I expected.

The lights flick on as the class comes to an end, and the redhead next to me keeps talking. This would usually annoy me, considering this is a class of peace, but she sounds friendly enough and somewhere in her chat session—where she did the majority of the chatting—she actually invited me out for a drink tonight. Since I don't know anyone, it sounds like a pretty great idea.

"Okay, so the bar is called The Black Alcove, have you heard of it?" she asks, spraying down her yoga mat and passing me the bottle.

"I think it's near my apartment," I answer honestly, even though about eight percent of me isn't sure it's the same bar I saw earlier.

"You think?" she laughs. "Where do you live?"

"In the Hillman Apartments on Center Street."

The redhead stops rolling her mat and her eyes go wide as she looks at me.

"Seriously! That's the building next to mine!"

This time it's me who pauses mid-roll. It's always hard moving to a new place, especially alone. My fear is that at twenty-one I've hit that awkward age where one, a person has all the friends they need, or two, they're making new friends in college, or three, there's something wrong with them. Seeing as college isn't something I want to do right away, I've been dreading that I'll end up as option three. Only the redhead here doesn't seem to have the same plan for me. I should probably ask her name.

"Well, neighbor, how about we actually introduce ourselves? I'm Alex." Like I was taught at a young age, I offer my hand and present her with a smile. She laughs it off but doesn't shake my hand.

"You're one of those polite, fancy girls, aren't you?" She eyes me, tucking her mat into her bag. "You're from the south. I hear the catch of an accent."

"Yeah, North Carolina."

"How in the heck did you end up in Wyoming?"

She isn't looking at me now, which is good. She seems like the outspoken type, and I've been told I have a "give-away" face. People always know what I'm thinking with just one look. And right now, I worry she might see the real answer and not accept the one I tell people, because once people learn you grew up in the foster system, they look at you differently. Most people don't realize they're doing it, looking at you with pity. Besides, I think telling someone I grew up without my real family and I came here to find my real brother might be a bit much for day one, or any day, really.

"Just trying something new." I shrug. I've got my yoga mat against my hip and my water bottle dangling from my finger as I wait for her.

"You know, I have a hunch the blond girl in the corner is new, too, because in this town almost everyone knows everyone and I do not know her. That, and college kids won't be rolling in for a few more months, sooo …" Red hair whips her neck around as she surveys the room. "Where is she?"

Her back straightens when she finds who she's looking for.

"Hey you," she hollers at a thin, pale blonde across the room. "Are you new here?"

The girl nods hesitantly, as though it caught her off guard

that someone would actually be talking to her. I know the look because I used to give it all the time.

"Are you twenty-one?"

The girl nods again.

"Fantastic, come have a drink with us tonight. My other girlfriends are all married with kids now; I need a couple new single gals. What's your name?"

"Skylar," the blonde answers, still seeming a little unsure of my new redheaded friend. Crud, what is her name?

"And you are?" I ask, urging her one more time to share her name.

"Beth." She laughs. "Sorry I got a little sidetracked when you asked me earlier."

I notice how Skylar returns her mat to the pile of borrowed ones, and then she thanks the instructor. Beth and I thank her as well before we step out in the hallway where cool air brushes against my skin now wet from sweat.

"Alright, so let's all go home and shower and meet at the BA in about an hour?" Beth looks between me and Skylar. It's actually cute that she is all about this new friend thing. I want to know more about these friends she used to hang around, but without knowing whether it's a sore subject or not, I better not.

"Alex, we can walk together if you want. Skylar, do you know where to go?"

Skylar nods and then turns for the locker room while Beth and I head for the exit. We part ways, and as I drive to my new apartment, I mentally cross my fingers that I don't reveal too much during drinks. Sharing little pieces of your life with a new friend is usually what happens when you meet someone new. And no one wants to know that, for years, I'd thought my family didn't want me. That's why I was in the foster system, right? Because someone didn't want to be my parent or devote enough of their time to me.

At this time, letting anyone in on this secret is not something I want to do. I have no idea why I was ready to move to another state but not ready to admit to anyone that I'm really here. That gut-aching feeling that there could be a chance he's changed his mind won't go away, and until it does, this is my secret to keep.

I take a quick shower and dry my hair before putting on a pair of jeans with holes down the front—sadly they weren't made that way, but I've managed to alter them to at least look fashionable—and a new t-shirt. It's only June and I've only been here since this morning, but I swear I've already gone through the chilly morning, a warm and misleading afternoon, and now, it's turning into a windy evening. The weather here can't seem to make up its mind.

I steal a glance at the clock on my phone. I told Beth I'd meet her outside about forty-five minutes after we left the gym. It's about that time, and although I should stay home to unpack some things, I rush out the door to find her standing on the sidewalk, chatting away on her phone. She, too, is wearing a pair of jeans, only hers are sans the holes and she's got on a green hoodie that makes her red hair even brighter than before.

"Perfect timing because I am starving," she says dramatically, but in a fun way. I'm learning that Beth is one of those beautiful outspoken women. The kind that are unaware of how attractive they are. Not that I'm attracted to her, but her personality is attractive, and that I do enjoy. I sort of hope a bit of her bluntness can rub off on me one day.

We walk to the bar, passing the time with small chitchat—age, birthdays, music, all the random things. She's twenty-four while I'm twenty-one. Her birthday is in January, mine is in October, both on the twenty-third of the month, which we find pretty coincidental. And we both feel the same about music: as long as it's good, the genre doesn't matter. It isn't until we reach the bar that she tells me she also works here, so I shouldn't be thrown off when every employee stops by the table to say "hey."

Only two tables are open when we arrive, and there isn't a spot open at the bar. Beth rushes to a booth, motioning for me to follow her.

"It's still early, but the burgers here are to die for. Once people eat their dinner, it will die down till the evening rush," she tells me, sliding a menu my way.

I'm about to open it when the door opens and Skylar walks in. Like earlier, she hesitates before she steps inside. When she catches the sight of Beth's hand waving in the air to gain her attention, she heads right for our table without even a glance at anyone as she passes them.

"Thanks for inviting me," she says, taking a seat next to Beth. "I actually ate right before yoga, so I hope it's okay that I just came to hang out. I don't really know anyone here." She starts to bite her nails, looking nervously back and forth between Beth and myself.

"I just moved here, too. Today actually," I say, hoping to calm her nerves. Her hand drops and she sits up a little straighter.

"Oh, you two are cute." Beth laughs. "If you want to know people, I can help you with that. But first, pick out some food so we can order."

We sit in silence as we each look over the menu. I haven't read even two items before three different people stop by to say hi. Beth doesn't introduce us to any of them. I guess these aren't the people she wants us to know.

"Hey, Beth," a small female with a blonde and brown fade says as she stops at our booth.

"Abby." Beth doesn't even glance up to look at her.

Abby stands there, not acting offended as she offers both me and Skylar a fake smile. It's a little awkward.

"Can I get you something to drink?"

"I'll just have water," Skylar says quickly.

"Can I have a Roy Rogers?" I ask. Abby stares at me while Beth laughs.

"I thought we were coming out for a drink. Water and a Roy Rogers are not what I meant."

"Hey, I need to eat first," I say and this seems to an acceptable answer. Beth orders a Redds' Apple Ale, and the moment Abby shifts away from the table, I have a direct view of the bar. More specifically, of the guy standing behind the bar. It's my neighbor. He's on my shit list for breaking the only thing I had left to remind me of my brother, but right now I'm realizing something else: there is a stupid crazy hot guy living next door to me and I can't pull my eyes away. He flashes a smile at the two women in front of him and then he winks. His gaze lifts, finding mine. With a tilt of his head and another cute-as-hell grin, he waves at me.

"Oh, I see you've found Conner," Beth says.

"The guy behind the bar?" I ask, trying to sound uninterested.

"That's the one. If he weren't my best friend's little

brother, I'd probably look at him with lust-filled eyes the way you are now."

"I am not." I laugh off her comment.

"It's true, and I think the fact he has a son he spends almost every free moment with makes women even more interested."

"Jake?" I ask, thinking of the little brown-haired boy I met earlier today.

"How did you know?" Beth asks.

"I met him earlier today."

"Oh that's right, you two are neighbors. Well, dang, I bet things around here are about to get pretty interesting."

"Why?" I ask, my eyes searching him out once again. But he's gone now. It's for the best. I shouldn't be checking him out. Where there is a cute guy and a kid, there is mother and significant other. I'm many things—a runner, a reader, a dreamer, even a hopeless romantic—but a home-wrecker, I am not.

"I'm no guy, but if I had a girl like you living across from me, practically there when I came home at night, I'd try to do something about it."

"Oh," I laugh her comment off once again. "I'm not in that place right now." It's true. This isn't the time for me to be starting a relationship with anyone. I mean, I've grown up in multiple foster homes, and each time I thought I found my place, they up and rejected me, placing me in a new home. Trust in the everyday human isn't something I have, and if I can't even put it in this brother who is looking for me, as much as I want to, I sure as heck know I can't put it in this random guy who already has a family. Why am I even thinking about this? Being hot is no excuse for having no manners. Which, after our encounter earlier, he is clearly lacking.

"Seriously? When isn't a girl in the place for a hot guy?"

"I've just got some other things going on my life right now that don't have place for a guy. Especially one who is—"

"Smoking hot," Skylar says, reminding me she's at the table, too.

Beth is about to object to me or agree with Skylar, I assume, when a tall figure appears at our table. My attention is pulled to focus on him. He has these deep dark brown eyes that I've never seen before but would be perfectly fine looking at for the rest of my life. My heart beats faster as I continue to check him. Dark hair just long enough to run your hands through. Strong, defined cheekbones with dark, perfectly shaved facial hair makes him look dreamy. All features I must have missed earlier in the hallway.

His chest rises and falls, grabbing my attention. The black t-shirt he's wearing reads The Black Alcove in white letters just about the chest pocket. I try to keep my attention here instead of near his eyes, because the heated look he's flashing my way right now is exciting something inside me.

"Ladies," he says, now sharing his grin with the rest of the table. "Beth, I didn't realize you had more friends." There's a joking tone to his voice that I find adorable. *No. No, I don't find it adorable.*

"Ha funny, Conner, this is Skylar." Skylar waves but doesn't look up. "And you already know Alex."

"Well, I met her briefly today, yes." He switches his gaze from hers to mine. "I actually came over here to apologize. I'm sorry about earlier, and I hope you got everything else moved in okay."

"I did, thank you," I answer, managing to turn my gaze to a plastic beer advertisement on the table.

"Actually, she was just telling me how she needs to move some furniture around, but some pieces are too heavy. Since you're her neighbor, you might be able to help."

I don't need to be looking at myself to know that my eyes have grown and my jaw is hanging open slightly at the lie. Her brow rises as she tilts her head toward Conner. I've changed my mind—Beth's bluntness isn't an admirable trait.

"I'd be happy to help," Conner says before I can correct her.

"That's really not necessary. I'll be fine."

"Well, it's not like I have to go out of my way. I get off around ten tonight, and if that's too late I can come by tomorrow afternoon."

"Tomorrow afternoon. We already have plans after this," Beth adds quickly, taking a notepad out of Conner's pocket and writing something down. Hopefully, this said cheeseburger.

"I'll see you tomorrow, then." His eyes have found mine once again, leaving me speechless. I nod as he walks away.

"Yeah, okay, I'm just going to say right now, with that dreamy look on your face, that place you're in … well, I think it just opened up a spot for Conner. Oh, and after we eat, we're all going to your place because that furniture isn't going to misplace itself."

"Where were you when I was in high school?" Skylar smiles as she plays with the napkin her water is sitting on. "And whatever he did, with a smile like his, I'd have forgiven him already."

The two quickly go into high-school talk. I shrug off the

topic of my neighbor, because, if anything, I really do need help moving my TV stand and I guess I should make nice if I'm going to continue living here. I don't have to even make friends with him, just be polite is all. Conner and I are nothing but neighbors.

CHAPTER TWO

Conner

It's been way too long since I've been alone with anyone of the opposite gender. It shouldn't make me all clammy hands nervous, but it does. I've forgotten what it feels like to be attracted to someone. I need to man up quick before I make it obvious to the entire world, or worse, before I make it obvious to Alex and make a fool of myself more than I already have with her.

"Are you really going over to that girl's apartment tomorrow?" Abby asks as I wipe down the bar. We make eye contact and I can see it right away she isn't too happy with the idea. I'm pretty sure that ever since she lived with Logan and me last summer—lesson learned on that move—she's had this idea that something would happen between the two of us. I've made sure I'm always on my best behavior so as to not lead her on, and I think I do fairly well with it, but still, she looks hurt right now.

"I'm just moving some furniture, and she lives across the

hall from me. It's not like I'm going out of my way to see her. You should know just as well as everyone else who knows me that I don't jump into anything that involves a woman."

"Yeah, but I'm sure you still have needs that you need taken care of."

Suddenly, the idea of Alex on her back with her long legs wrapped around my waist raises my heart rate. A benefits kind of thing isn't the worst idea, and her living in the same building makes things less complicated. Shit, I should be trying to think of Heather like this, not some woman I just met.

Abby clears her throat, and when I glance at her, her eyes are narrowed at me. That probably isn't where her mind was going with the suggestion, and it sure isn't where my mind needs to be when I just told another woman we could give it a go. Although, that area of my life isn't going too well either. Alex's movers took so long that I had to cancel on Heather. She wasn't happy with me. I knew that the moment I dropped Jake off at her place and the only word she said to me was "thanks." I guess telling her "yeah, let's try this" and then canceling our first date wasn't the best way to start.

"You boys are all the same." Abby rolls her eyes and stomps away.

My friend and the other bartender of the night, Lucas, gives me the nod that I'm good to go. My heart rate immediately picks up pace. I can do this. I need to stop acting like a pansy. Women are not something I should be afraid of.

The weather is still warm when I step outside, and for a moment I contemplate taking my time to get home. I rode my bike to work, which sounds lame, but I used to ride all the time. Trails were my favorite, but I haven't had the time lately. I should get Jake a bike and we could go together.

So I peddle slowly, to enjoy the night. When I pull up in front of our building, the light to Alex's apartment is shining brightly through the windows that at this moment, don't have curtains hung over them yet. Like my apartment, we both have a three-sectioned window in the front, the center being the largest. The windows are large enough that if you pop the screen out, you could step out onto the grass without a struggle. I know because I tried it once when I set up a trap for anyone who thinks they can break into my home where my son lives.

I'm about to push my bike inside the building and leave it in the hallway like I occasionally do when a voice that isn't the radio singing comes from her apartment. She can't hit a note at all, and it makes me laugh. I lean back and, like a creeper, look into her apartment. She has her back to me as she hangs a painting on the wall. Her voice is now louder than … Taylor Swift, is it? and her ass is bopping from side to side. She seems to be enjoying herself—at least she's in a good mood even at ten o'clock at night.

Still listening to her sing, I lean my bike against the wall and head into my apartment for a quick shower. The warm water splashes against my skin, and I absorb the clean feeling it gives me. Like everything that happened today can be washed away and I can give it fresh start tomorrow. I could really use a fresh start with Alex ... and Heather, for that matter.

By the time I crawl into bed, I've planned my day out for tomorrow. First thing, I'll go next door and apologize once again because I don't think she really accepted the one I gave her this evening. After that, I'll see if Heather and Jake can do lunch, and then I'll help move some furniture and be back for another shift at the BA. Hopefully, I won't piss anyone off the way I did today.

* * *

The next morning, I knock on Alex's door as I head out to meet Heather and Jake for brunch. There isn't any music playing like last night, so it's easy for me to hear as her bare feet trudge against the hard floors inside her apartment to open the door.

Her hair is down today, falling in waves over her shoulders. She's wearing a longer pink tank top that is bunched at the side and black leggings that look painted on. We both stand there, eyes locked as we stare at the other.

"I thought you weren't coming by until this afternoon?" she asks, breaking eye contact and stepping back to let me in.

I remain in the doorway.

"I am. I just wanted to stop by and apologize once again."

She leans against the frame, giving me more attention than she did last night at the bar.

"I don't normally act like that, and I am really sorry I took whatever was bothering me out on you. It was unnecessary, and had I acted like a gentleman, the way my mother taught me, there is a good chance I wouldn't have broken something of yours."

A small smile appears at the left corner of her lips.

"I'd like to replace it," I add.

"You can't, but you can start making it up to me by helping me move my TV stand." Her voice is perkier this time, and she sounds pleased to actually be speaking to me. I like this side of my new neighbor.

"Yeah, I'll do that first thing when I get back," I say, smiling and stepping away.

"Oh, you're headed out?" The smile I almost had out of her is gone.

"I'm going to meet my son and his mother right now. I'll be back after that to do anything you want me to do."

A blank expression takes over her face and she crosses her arms.

"Don't bother. Thanks anyway," she says and closes the door in my face.

What just happened?

I don't have enough time to think it over before I receive a text from Heather to tell me she and Jake are out front.

Okay, I had better shake this off. All my focus needs be on Heather and Jake now.

"Hey," I say as I slide into the passenger's seat of Heather's Ford Explorer. "How is everyone today?"

"Dad!" Jake cheers from the back seat. "Mom said I could have pancakes today!"

I can feel my smile grow at his enthusiasm.

"That's what I'm going to have, too," I tell him.

"He's been wired since you dropped him off yesterday. I'm not sure syrup or anything with sugar is a good idea for him," Heather says, glaring at me.

"Oh, he'll be fine," I reply as she pulls onto the road.

"You're not the one who has to hang out with him all day."

I cringe at the way she says *has*. Almost as though she's being forced to spend time with our son.

"I would if you let him stay with me more often," I say, stating the obvious.

"And I would if you didn't have such a busy schedule, Conner."

"I have a busy schedule because I'm doing everything you've insisted I do to earn more time with Jake."

"Oh, so working hard and being a good example isn't something you want for Jake," she argues back, her voice growing louder.

"That's a fancy way to spin my words. Let's talk about this later when Jake isn't around us."

"I should turn around."

"Why?" Why does a simple disagreement get her worked up?

"We clearly can't even get along on a car ride to a restaurant. This will never work."

"You just want to give up then?" I ask.

"No, but we're already fighting."

"Let's go eat and enjoy our time together," I suggest, knowing she is giving me an out that I should be taking. But I said I'd do anything for Jake, and I meant it.

"You're sure?" Heather asks again.

"Yes."

The remainder of the drive is silent, and Heather and I don't exchange much conversation as we eat other than determine the next time Jake will stay with me. Jake does enough talking about the new Ninja Turtle episode he watched this morning to entertain us for the entire meal.

When she drops me off, I lean into the backseat to give Jake a hug goodbye. He waves out the window as she pulls away, and I take a seat on the steps outside the apartment building.

That plan I had to not piss anyone off today has officially failed. Here's hoping tomorrow is a better day.

Alexis

My neighbor is a total jackhole.

That's the perfect name for him, and I'll keep calling him that until he proves me wrong, which will probably never happen.

Crossing my legs as I sit in the center of my couch, I pull my computer onto my lap. I read somewhere once that a great way to avoid keeping emotions bottled up is to write them out, whether it's traditionally in a journal or typing it out on the computer. I could never make this a career because my thoughts are all over the place, but it really does help.

I spend a good thirty minutes writing about how the stress of imagining my brother and his wife—who I learned about by Googling him—rejecting me and not believing me when I say I'm his sister has me ready to break into tears at least five times a day. Just thinking about it gets me all choked up. Rejection will always be hard for me to accept. My family has never wanted me, and foster homes struggled to keep me— what makes me think anything is different now?

I snap my laptop shut and lace up my running shoes. I make it about a block from my apartment when I spot Skylar lying in the grass of the town central park.

"Do you always lie in the grass?" I ask, finding myself envious of how relaxed she looks just lying there, letting her body soak up the morning sun.

One eye pops open as she rises to her left elbow and cups her other hand over her eyes to guard them from the sun.

"When it's a nice day out like today, I do." She smiles. "Want to join me?"

Run in the sun or sit in the sun? Sit, definitely sit.

"Is that what you have planned for the rest of your day?" I ask, attempting small talk. Since I don't know her and have no idea if she has a past she doesn't want to talk about like I do, this is safe question.

"Maybe. I heard there was a hiking trail on the mountain. Thought I might check it out," she says. We both turn our view to the mountains behind us. They aren't big by any means, but they are still mountains.

"That's sounds fun," I say, inviting myself.

Skylar laughs and pushes herself off the ground. "I just need to swing by the gym and grab my gym shoes. I keep them in the locker there. Then we can go. You have a car, right, to drive us?"

"Yes and yes." I stand next to her. "Meet you at the gym in ten minutes?"

"Okay." Skylar sets off right away and I jog back to my place. So I went out for a run and now I'm going hiking. A spontaneous day like this is just what I need.

I run inside, grab my keys and purse, and fill a water bottle. Skylar is waiting outside when I get to the gym.

"I got directions from the girl inside," she says as she gets in.

We drive, turning on each road the girl at the gym wrote down on this white piece of paper, and it surprisingly only takes us less than another ten minutes to get to the trail.

I close my car door and look around after I've parked.

Cars are lining the road in and out of the area. Water falls somewhere behind me, and I spot the start to few different rocky trials between cracks in the trees. Picnic tables are set up down a path that lines up with the road we drove in on.

"This must be a popular place," I say.

"Looks like it. Oh, there's a sign. I bet all those colors are trail markings."

Sure enough, from the sign we learn there is one big trail, but you can mix up the paths to shorten the hike or extend it. Since neither of us have anything to do, we agree on the long path.

Halfway up the first hill, I stop.

"This … is … harder … than I thought," I say, trying to catch my breath and taking a sip of my water. Skylar sits on boulder that marks a turning point of the trail. "I thought I was in better shape than this."

"I should have brought water," she says and I offer her mine.

"Drink as much as you need."

We finish catching our breath and hike for maybe another five minutes before we stop again.

"What is this? I don't understand how out of shape I am," Skylar says.

"Me either. I was always an active kid. I ran track and was always playing outdoors with the other kids, growing up. It makes no sense," I reply.

"I've had a personal trainer most of my life, I should be prepared for this." She laughs.

"A personal trainer? Nothing about you screams you need help to stay in shape."

"Mom insisted I always look my best," she says.

The last word comes out more quietly than the rest. I wait, not sure what I should do because we are coming really close to talking about our past, and by the way she's focusing on the greenery of the mountains, I'd say she doesn't want to talk about it either.

"You girls doing okay?"

We both turn to the deep, masculine voice. A man with cropped blonde hair, waves of abs and muscles—since his shirt is tucked into the back of his shorts, everything is very visible—and sweat displaying droplets over his core is staring down at us. I almost get to enjoy ogling him, but my damn jackhole neighbor steps up behind him, looking like this guy's clone, ripped abs and all.

"Seriously," I groan, crossing my arms and glaring at Conner.

Blonde guy chuckles. "Is this the neighbor?"

"Yeah, I told you every time she sees me, it's like I've ruined her day."

"Considering I've known you for two days, yes, you have ruined my great mood both days. Skylar, let's go."

"I broke one thing and you're going to hate me forever?" Conner calls out as we walk away. I don't know about Skylar, but I'm doing a fine job of pretending to be in great shape with my speed walk uphill right now.

"Fine. Ignore me! But unless you move, you're going to see me every day and you'll learn to like it."

Taking the bait, I turn around and stomp back to him.

He's grinning and it looks good on him, but I can't let him know I think that.

"Just because we live across the hall from each other doesn't mean we have to see each other."

"Hang out with me once, and then if you really, absolutely don't enjoy it, I'll politely ignore you and you can ignore me back anytime we see each other in the hall."

"No." I laugh.

"Oh come on, give the guy a chance," blond guy says.

Memories of stories I'd heard in the foster system, kids whose parents cheated or kids who didn't have a parent because they left the other for someone else, flash through my mind. Every kid will have a different story for a miserable childhood and a cheating parent might not be the reason, but it's one less reason I can help avoid. I will never be why a child doesn't get the parents and family they deserve. I don't need to know my neighbor to feel this way.

"And you are?" I snap. Skylar comes into view from the corner of my eye.

"I'm Lucas, and I think you should give him a shot. I'm not just saying that because he's my friend. I'm saying that because you should never judge someone before you know them."

"You don't know anything about me, so you don't get to make that assumption," I say to him then look at Conner. "You have better things to focus on, so stop wasting my time."

This time when Skylar and I walk away he doesn't yell anything. If all men in this town act like those two, maybe I should leave and never meet my brother. What if he hangs out with people like Lucas and Conner?

This move is starting to look like a very bad decision on my part.

CHAPTER THREE

Alexis

The next morning comes fast as I awake to my ringing cell phone. Beth's name flashes across the screen and I immediately love/hate the fact I met her. Love it because, so far, she is pretty awesome, and hate it because I like to sleep in and she apparently does not.

"Hello?" my groggy voice greets her.

"Hey girl, rise and shine. I'm on my way over and we're headed to the lake! I ran into Sky last night at the gym and she said there is a good chance you'd be free today since you're still waiting to see if you got that job."

"What time is it?" I roll over and see eight a.m. in bright red letters on my alarm clock.

"It's time for you to get out of bed and get ready. I'll meet you outside in an hour."

I don't have a chance to negotiate more time, not that I should need it, or object to going to the lake, not that I would, before she hangs up her end of the call.

An hour later I'm dressed, I've eaten toast again because I need to go grocery shopping, and I'm stepping outside the moment I see a green nitro pull up to the curb. Beth waves from the window. As I walk to her car, I notice that Conner's truck is gone. I'm basically on the sidewalk, so the chances of running in to him are already slim, but knowing he isn't even here to chance a run-in is nice.

I'm about 98 percent sure he was flirting with me yesterday morning right before he left to meet his son and his son's mother. The worst part is, I started to fall for it, and I actually for a split second thought I misjudged him. Seeing him when I was with Skylar was just as awful. I don't feel bad for turning him down, but I do feel like I should have handled the way I spoke to him better.

This is ridiculous. I need a day away from my apartment already just to clear my head. Why am I still obsessing over my jackhole neighbor?

Paramore fills my ears as I open the passenger door and get in. Beth is texting away on her cell phone, but she still greets me.

"Hey girl," she says without looking up.

"Don't you know it's nine in the morning? You've got this radio turned up like we're about to go out on the town partying," I say, turning the music down.

"Hey." She snaps her view toward me and cocks her head. "Don't be turning my radio down like we've been friends forever. We only just met yesterday." A smile slowly appears and she twists the dial to the right.

"Okay, new friend, what am I allowed to do in your car? And how far away is this said lake?" I ask. I'm waiting for the gym to tell me whether or not. I assume they won't call me back this soon, but I want to be available and not out of service just in case they do.

"It's about a twenty-, thirty-minute ride. Nothing too intense," she answers, placing the car in gear and pulling away from the curb. "And what you can do in my car this time is tell me all about your afternoon with Conner yesterday."

"I'd rather not. Plus, it was more of an encounter. Not an afternoon."

"Oh, come on, it couldn't have been that bad."

"It wasn't that bad, but I still don't want to talk about it."

"Hmm, did he hit on you?"

"Beth," I say with a warning tone. Although it clearly wasn't intimidating enough because she goes on as if I didn't say anything at all.

"He did, didn't he?" Her fingers tap on the steering wheel. "I can't believe he did it. I have to give the guy some credit though. Impressive."

What does she mean, impressive? There is nothing impressive about a guy who is willing and openly showing that he would cheat on his girlfriend or whatever they are.

"You might be into that sort of behavior, but I am definitely not. It's repulsive and completely disrespectful."

With my feet on the dashboard, I cross my arms and look out the window. I like Beth and she's the only person I know in this town besides Skylar, so I'll probably let this topic go, but it still sucks that she is pro cheaters.

"Whoa, okay, first, although I am a fan of the feet dashboard position, it's totally unsafe." She stares at me until my flip-flops are safely back on the mat. "And second, are you telling me you didn't enjoy Conner hitting on you?"

"That's exactly what I'm saying."

"Sooo, does this mean you're into women? Because it's totally cool if you are."

"What are you talking about?" By the yikes frown she has on her face, I'm going to assume that whatever look I have going on right now is giving her the answer.

"Okay, whoops, my bad. I must have missed something. What's so wrong with him flirting with you?'

I take a moment before I answer her. There is a reason she is so interested in whether I'm attracted to Conner. Maybe Jake's mother is a bad egg. Still, nothing is a good enough reason to cheat.

"Nothing about being the other woman excites me, therefore his flirting is fully repulsive."

When Beth doesn't respond right away, I'm relieved that the conversation is over. But no, I was premature with that assumption. She erupts into laughter.

I don't join her. What sort of friendship have I've gotten myself into? Beth really is a different person.

"What's so funny?" I finally ask.

"Well, to start, Jake's mother is not in the picture. They are sharing custody right now. Conner only gets every other weekend and occasionally during the week when Heather lets him."

Conner is single.

"By the lusty look you have going on again right now, I'd say I've just made your day."

"I don't feel bad about ogling him anymore, is all. Still, I told you the other night, I'm not in that place right now." Pretending to not be ready for a relationship is a much safer route than saying I came here for another guy, my brother to be exact, who hasn't seen or heard from me in more than fifteen years.

"You might not think it's the right time, but the world may have another plan for you,"

I laugh at this both because I really enjoy the way she speaks her mind and also because what was a serious conversation turned into a pretty good one. One thing is for sure: I owe Conner an apology for the way I acted yesterday. If I thought he had no manners, I must look ten times worse.

"I was kind of rude to Conner yesterday," I admit.

"That's okay. He probably thought it was hot."

"What?"

"I'm joking. Just say sorry and explain what happened. Conner is one of the most understanding people I know. He has to be, what with the cards life has dealt him."

"What do you mean?"

Her car starts to slow down as we turn, passing a sign welcoming us to the lake. We wind around turns and go up and down a few hills until a beautiful lake surrounded by the red hills and sandy beaches comes into view. We pass a marina, a boat club, and many lake houses. Now, I've seen the ocean and been on a boat, but a lake is new for me. I watch as a neon green boat jets across the open water before I realize Beth is speaking.

"I think I've told you enough about Conner. You should get to know him and let him answer these questions for himself. I only know what Sara has told me, and being the best friend's wife doesn't exactly mean she knows the facts to a T."

Sara? My sister-in-law's name is Sara.

"Sara who?" I ask, all thoughts of Conner and me gone.

"Sara Parker. She owns the bar Conner and I work at with her husband," Beth says as she parks the car. It takes me a moment for me to look away. She knows my brother. Conner knows my brother. She said they were best friends. I could run into Logan by hanging out with these people. I should go. I need to go.

"Hey, are you okay? You look a little pale."

"I'm fine," I answer quickly, opening the door. Fresh air should help. I can't ask her to take me back home now—that would lead to too many questions.

I stumble out, grabbing my bag and swinging it over my shoulder. Cool air hits my face and I shiver. Is this the type of weather they go to the lake in?

"Are you going to be okay walking to boat on your own? I need to grab my cooler."

I nod.

I can feel her eyes watching me. "We going right over there, to the boat Conner is next to."

What?

Sure enough, Conner is squatting beside a boat in all his sexy glory. He's got on a pair of swim trunks that fall to his knees and a cut-off blue shirt that reads HYPERLITE across the chest. He looks up then, as if he knows I am watching him, and waves.

With my head held high and pretending I didn't just learn a lot of new facts to overwhelm me, enough to fear that I could be meeting my brother today, I head in Conner's direction, completely unprepared for whatever this day decides to bring at me.

· · ·

Conner

I can't for the life of me figure out what—other than breaking a picture frame—I did to piss Alex off so much. The way she acted when Lucas and I ran into her and her friend on our run yesterday made it clear she doesn't like me. I lost too much sleep over it, and when I woke this morning I made the decision to just let it go. So she doesn't like me. Who cares? I have the people I need and want in my life, and they are the people I need to give my focus.

But I didn't prepare myself to see her again so soon, so everything I decided is now shattered. I'm attracted to her, damn it, no matter how snippy she can get with me.

The way her eyes are frozen to mine, not moving with each step she takes makes my heart race. I swallow as I tear my gaze away to check her out. She has those same cut-off jean shorts on, a pink t-shirt with the word LOVE written across it in big silver letters, and a simple pair of black flip-flops. Her hair curls over her shoulders and down her back. The sun shines off it, providing a glow. I lick my lips, bringing moisture back to my dry mouth. Whatever this tingling feeling she's causing in me, I need to be rid of it because she can see it.

"Hey, Conner," she says, stopping in front of me. I continue tying the knot I've been working on for at least two minutes thanks to her distraction, and I finally secure the boat against the dock until the others get here.

"Hey," I say.

"I didn't know you had a boat," she says with a half smile.

"It's my parents'. Beth asked the other night before you all left the BA if we could take it out."

"Well, that was nice of you."

Our already awkward conversation comes to a halt. It's not that I don't want to talk to her, but she's made it very clear I'm not her favorite person. I'm not going to act like everything is fine just because she decides she wants to talk now.

I hop into the boat, leaving her standing on the dock. Without making it obvious as I pull out some lifejackets to have handy, I sneak a few glances her way. Her hands are curling and uncurling as she looks all around her. Then she steps onto the boat.

"Look, Conner, I'm sorry about the way I acted yesterday. I know I didn't make a good impression, but I have a very good reason." Her voice has perked up and sparked my curiosity.

"Go on," I say when it's clear she's waiting for a response.

"See, I thought after I met you that … well, I assumed that you …"

"You assumed what?" I ask, not understanding what she's trying to tell me but finding myself curious as to what could make her this nervous.

"I just thought you were involved with someone was all, but Beth set me straight and I'm sorry."

I grin. "And you were upset you thought I was taken?"

"No." She looks away. I catch the spark of smile before she's looking fully in the other direction. "You dropped a box of my things and broke something special to me, so for that I was upset. My behavior yesterday was purely because I assumed the worst in you when it came to your family, and that was wrong of me."

Her head drops to her chin as she plays with the bottom of her t-shirt. The emotion she just displayed toward family grabs at my chest. Then she looks at me with her eyes sparkling, and I'm at a loss for words. I find them though, because I can't pass up the moment.

"Maybe if you take me up on my dinner invite, we can get to know each other a little better and you can learn firsthand that I'm not that kind of guy."

"And what kind of guy are you?" she asks. She is damn cute when she flirts. I take a step toward her.

"Come over for dinner tonight and find out."

Her gaze flutters over my body, sending another tingle throughout every inch. The urge to lean forward and press my lips to hers takes over. The second her eyes are on my mouth, she touches her lips. My mind doesn't have time to process what I'm about to do. I step toward her and dip my head. My timing, however, couldn't be worse.

"We're here!" Ethan says loudly, clearing his throat right before my lips have a chance to touch Alex's. She jumps at the sudden interruption, allowing her body to fall closer to mine. As if I've done it a million times before, my hand reaches out to steady her at the small of her back. She blushes and looks away.

A squeal and tiny feet running along the dock catch my attention. I lunge forward, swooping my niece right off her feet as I pull her into the boat. She screams and laughs at the same time. I've still got ahold of her, and because she already has her pink Minnie Mouse life vest on, I'm about to fake dip her into the water when my sister walks up.

"Conner Davis Brian, don't you even think about it! The water is too cold for her to be in it." Her mom voice is spot on today. Clara looks up at me, her little chin ducking into her vest as I set her on the floor of the boat.

"Alex, this is one of my good friends, Ethan, and his wife,

also known as my sister, Kelsey. Kelsey and Ethan, this is Alex. She just moved into the apartment across from mine." I hold out a hand to help my sister on the boat while Ethan starts to spray sunscreen on Clara.

"Older sister, smarter sister, I'm one in the same." Kelsey shakes her hand. "It's nice to meet you."

"It's nice to meet you, too," Alex says, and I can't help but enjoy the smile on her face. Ethan extends his hand as well. They, too, shake but Ethan doesn't let go.

"Have I met you before?" he asks.

"No, I don't think so."

"Are you sure? You look really familiar."

"She just moved here from …" I pause because I don't know the answer to what I was saying.

"North Carolina," she finishes for me and a little bit of her accent comes out.

"Huh, that's just crazy. You seriously look like someone I know."

"Ethan, stop freaking her out," my sister says. "What is taking Beth so long?"

Ethan finally lets go of Alex's hand and takes a seat next to Kelsey at the back of the boat. He leans over, whispering something in her ear, and my sister's eyes quickly dart up to Alex. I'll have to ask him about this later.

"Should you be in the boat?" I ask my sister, changing the subject.

"I asked the same thing," Ethan answers for her. "Yes, she can, so let's just leave it at that."

"I wasn't that mean."

Ethan's brows rise.

"I wasn't."

My sister laughs.

I shake my head, laughing silently with my sister, when I catch Alex's movement to my left. She's sitting down now, leaned forward, digging in her bag. Her shirt inches up in the back, revealing the top of her bright yellow bikini. Now I can't wait to see what she looks like in a bathing suit. *Come on sun, warm up.*

Beth finally joins us, pulling her cooler behind her by the handle. Ethan helps her load it, and everyone takes their seats as I untie the boat and pull away.

We spend the morning cruising around the lake, showing Alex the local beaches.

Once lunch comes around, we take the boat into the canyon and let it sit idle while we eat the sandwiches my sister brought.

"So what brings you to Wind Valley?" my sister asks the moment the engine is off.

"Just something new," Alex answers.

"Yeah, this must be quite the change up. Are you working anywhere?"

"I applied at the gym, near the east side of town as I heard someone call it."

"Oh, Conner works out there," Ethan says.

"Can you make enough money working there?" Kelsey shoots off another question, and I have to grind my teeth together to keep myself from looking like the rudest guy on earth by snapping at my sister. Mom and Dad never taught us to be this nosy.

"Okay, that's enough of the twenty questions for Alex," I interrupt, taking a more mature route and reaching for a can of Pringles, offering them to Alex. She mouths "thank you" and takes one. I know she wasn't thanking me for the chips.

"I'm sorry. I just wanted to know more about the girl who's dating my brother, is all."

"Oh, we're not dating," Alex replies right away.

The word "yet" is on the tip of my tongue, and the idea sinks my stomach. I'm supposed to be trying with Heather, and yet one good interaction with Alex has my mind in a jam.

"Oh, from what I saw earlier, I just assumed," Kelsey adds.

"Why couldn't Sara and Logan make it again?" Beth finally speaks up. She's been glued to her phone all afternoon. It usually bothers me when people are more focused on their phone than spending time with their friends, but right now, I'm thankful she wasn't paying attention and successfully changed the subject without it coming off as too obvious.

"Sara had an appointment today, and Logan, as usual, went with her."

"I still can't believe both my best friends are having kids. Thank goodness I met you when I did, Alex."

Because I haven't been able to stop since she admitted why she was acting so standoffish before today, I smile at Alex. I expect her to be happy about Beth's comment. Well, I guess I expected anything other than watery eyes.

"Are you okay?" I ask, getting up to kneel in front of her. I grab her hand as she waves the other in front of her eyes.

"I'm sorry, I don't know what came over me." She looks at Beth. "So your friend Sara, the one you mentioned earlier who owns the bar, she's having a baby?"

"Yep."

"Wow." Alex sounds a bit choked up. "That's awesome."

As if it's an afterthought, she congratulates my sister, too. Kelsey thanks her but is now watching Alex with an odd expression. The same odd one Ethan had earlier. It's a mixture of shock and happiness with a little bit of unease that does nothing but leave me worried that my family and friends are going to scare away the first girl I feel something for other than just wanting to get her into bed.

Luckily for me, Alex doesn't notice, and we manage to go another hour on the boat without my sister or Ethan asking her something personal. When she gets in Beth's car and they drive away, I feel like I'm in high school all over again, counting down the hours till our first date.

CHAPTER FOUR

Alexis

I'm starving, and since I've been keeping busy with making new friends, I still have no food in my apartment. I know that Conner invited me over for dinner, but today was mentally exhausting. Everyone I met loaded more information on me that I have to keep repeating it to make sure I have it all straight. Conner is my neighbor, and somewhere between despising him for forty-eight hours, then spending the day on the water with him, I've already developed a crush, despite the fact he also happens to be best friends with my brother, Logan. Logan and Sara own the bar that Conner and Beth work at. And I'm going to be an aunt.

My eyes immediately tear up. Logan went through all the same things I did and yet, here he is, creating the family we never had. If he can overcome the way we were raised, then I can too. I just don't know how. Logan would be the perfect person to ask, but now he's moving on. What will happen if I just come barging back into his life bringing up the past that he's possibly happily forgotten by now?

I slide on a pair of slippers as I pass the last two boxes that I should be unpacking instead of reading another book. I open the fridge and stare. How, of all things, have I not made time to go to the store? As much as I'm thrilled over the dinner invitation, especially knowing I'm not coming between anyone, I'm almost too worn from the day to be good company. I should tell him I can't make it and go pick something up from the store, but that smell of garlic bread starting to waft across the hall has me craving spaghetti.

Conner's door is ajar. I hesitantly take a step toward it, rethinking skipping out on dinner since he clearly cooked, when the very guy himself comes through the building's front door instead of his own. He's caught off guard to find me standing in my doorway.

"Hey," he says with such a lazy grin that I find myself smiling back too. "Were you looking for me?" He's wearing a simple gray pair of sweats and a plain t-shirt. Sans shoes.

"Yes, I was actually just going to step out for some groceries when it occurred to me that I don't know where the closest store is."

His chuckle is deep as he closes the door behind him. "Well, there is actually a place within walking distance, but it's getting late and they don't stay open past ten. If you leave now you'll probably make it just fine, but you'd miss the awesome dinner I made."

"Oh."

I feel his hot gaze wash over me as he steps around me. "I made pasta. How about we eat dinner tonight and then tomorrow we can go to the store?"

"We?"

"Yeah," he answers, walking into his apartment. He starts talking again, which means I have to follow him inside. "I need to go to the store too. So if I need to go and you need to go, we could go at the same time." He pauses to look over his shoulder as he pulls garlic bread out of the oven. "Unless, of course, you don't like to grocery shop with other people."

"I guess there's nothing wrong with that, but what makes you so sure you'll want to hang out with me again after tonight? I mean, I could be crazy and you're only minutes away from finding that out."

Pulling two plates from his cupboard, he flashes me a grin that warms my cheeks instantly. "What type of crazy are you talking about?"

Although he makes me nervous, it's as though my mind and lips have their own plan.

"What kind of crazy can you handle?"

Plate midair, he freezes and stares at me. My body is drawn to him. I take a step and so does he. Then my phone rings.

Brought out of my daze, I pull my phone out of my pocket. It's an unknown number. Normally I wouldn't answer it, but it could be the gym.

"Hello." I step into the hall as I see Conner dishing out our plates.

"Hi, is this Alexis?"

"This is," I answer, a little thrown because no one has called me by my full name in more than two years.

"This is Maggie from the gym. We would like to offer you the position, if you're still interested."

"I am, yes. That would fantastic."

"Great, can you start on Thursday? That's two days from now."

"Yes, I can."

"We'll see you at three in the afternoon."

"Perfect, thank you."

I hang up and feel a huge weight lift off my shoulders. I step back into Conner's apartment to find him sitting on the couch, both plates ready to go with a glass of milk on the coffee table in front of his plate and mine.

"My place is kind of a mess. I hope this is okay."

"It's great." I say, taking the seat next to him.

We eat in silence, probably because I am famished and because it is some damn good pasta. Before I know it, I'm leaning back against his couch, watching *The Hangover* on his television as though it were something I did each day. Conner stands, reaching for my plate.

"Oh, I can get these." I push off the couch and try to take his plate. He objects and grabs mine out of my hand.

"I don't invite beautiful women over just to watch them do the dishes. No way. If you want to clean up, next time dinner is at your place."

I think he just asked me out again.

"Okay. I should get going anyway." I don't want to intrude for too long.

"At least stay until the movie is over."

Again, I lean back and nod. *Sure, why not?*

"So I know my sister asked you this, but what made you pick Wind Valley to move to?"

This is a question for which I have a rehearsed answer.

"I opened up a map, picked a state then a town at random and here I am. I just wanted something different."

"I don't think I could ever do that. Not even before Jake. I've always liked knowing where I'm going and why."

"Jake is very sweet and polite. From my brief meeting with him, I can see you've done a great a job raising him." I switch the subject like I always do when the questions are about me.

Conner comes back to the living room, a sad smile on his face.

"Thanks, that's really nice to hear. We had a bit of a rough start, but things are going well now."

Somewhere in that sentence I pick up that there is bigger story than he's letting on. I know exactly how he feels, and because I wouldn't want him to do it to me, I don't pry.

"You should be proud" is what I say instead.

"He'll actually be back next weekend, and a friend of mine is having a barbeque at his new house. He isn't moved in yet. I think that's what the barbeque is for, kind of have people over and stuff before everything is moved in or maybe he's luring us over there to help him move. My sister and Beth will be there—you should come."

"Oh, I'm not sure."

"Come on, Logan and Sara won't mind."

That settles it. I'm definitely not going.

"I, uh, could be working." *Oh that's good, and could possibly be true.*

"You got the job?" Conner is clearly excited for me.

"Yeah, that was the phone call I got earlier."

"Well, congrats. We should celebrate. I have some wine or beer in here somewhere." He stands and begins to search the fridge. "I keep everything for the adults in back where Jake can't reach it."

He pokes his head around the fridge and smiles. "So, what'll it be, wine or beer?"

"Wine," I answer, knowing a drink isn't the smartest idea right now, not when I'm around Conner, but a glass of wine also sounds delicious. He ducks his head again and I hear cupboards open and close as he pours me a glass.

One glass of wine, that's it. No more. More than that and I'll start talking, and I can't have that happen.

Conner

My hand shakes as I pour her a glass of white wine. I've spent more time with her today, and it's been better than the last two days, so I should feel more comfortable around her and I do, yet my nerves are all over the place.

I let out a deep breath before I step into the living room. One of Jake's stuffed Ninja Turtles is lying in the corner, and I laugh inside. Of everything I did today, picking up my apartment should have been on the list.

"I see you like to take pictures of Jake." Alex points to a photo of us on the swing set in the park across the street.

"Have to keep track of the memories in more than just your head, you know. A picture can spark a dozen emotions, and, well … my kid has the cutest smile."

Alex laughs.

"He looks just like you, you know."

"I do."

"Could you tell even when he was a baby?"

I keep smiling, but it's hard to hold it strong. She's going to find out eventually; I may as well tell her now. It's not like it's some sort of secret.

"Actually, I didn't know I had a son until Jake was two years old."

Her lips part in shock and her hand lifts to rest over her chest. Her eyes flash around the room as if she's looking for her words. Logan does this, too; it must be more common than I thought.

"How?"

"His mother didn't tell me. We were a drunken one-night stand. My behavior from our night together turned her away from contacting me."

"Wow."

"Yeah, it was hard at first, but we have a pretty stable relationship now, and I'd never trade him for a thing. I just wish I could go back and get those first two years back."

"You would have kept him?" Her voice isn't asking in a way that she doubts me, but in a way that she looks up to me. It hits somewhere inside my chest and I find myself quickly taking a pull from my beer.

"I wouldn't have thought twice about it. I mean, he's a baby, a kid, and he should have had a father."

Her eyes tear up then she gulps down her entire glass.

"I guess you were right," she says once she's finished.

"Right about what?" I ask.

"Earlier you said you're not the type of guy I assumed you to be."

"What kind of guy was that again?"

"I feel horrible that I thought you were trying to cheat on Jake's mom with me. I actually thought you were the kind of guy who would pick a random chick over family."

"As long as you don't keep secrets from me, I'm the nicest guy ever." I chuckle, because, come on, nothing could be worse than keeping the fact someone fathered a child from someone. Alex, however, doesn't find my statement funny.

"I should get going." She stands and heads for the door. I stand, too, following after her. It hadn't crossed my mind until just now how badly I want to kiss her. If she leaves, I may miss my chance.

"Dinner was great, and I had fun hanging out with you today." Her smile pierces my heart, and without a second thought, I'm pulling her into my arms and hugging her. The second I realize what I'm doing, her body goes stiff, and I get the feeling I ruined our good day with just one move. But then I feel her arms around my waist and I don't let go. I kiss the top of her head and pull back.

"Goodnight, Alex, I enjoyed your company as well."

She blushes as she backs away, turning for her apartment. After her door is closed, I stand there for a moment. How can I possibly feel this attracted to someone I hardly know? And why, even though I know so little about her, do I feel as though I've known her forever?

My cell rings. Heather. Shit, I should be making this dinner effort with her.

"Hello?" I answer, concerned why she is calling me at ten at night.

"Hey, Conner, Jake can't sleep and says he needs to talk to you before he could try it again."

My heart grows.

"Put him on."

"Dad?"

"Hey, bud, can't sleep?"

"No. I forgot Donny."

I glance around for the stuffed turtle I saw earlier.

"Yeah, he's right here."

"Oh."

"Can I bring him to you tomorrow?" I ask, trying to make him feel better. He sleeps with him every night. Last night he must have been too tired to notice he was missing.

"I just thought I lost him. Can he sleep with you?"

"Sure thing," I say, completely honest.

"Okay, 'night Dad."

"'Night, buddy."

"I'm glad you picked up," Heather says after Jake gives her the phone.

"Me too. I didn't realize he was so attached to one stuffed animal."

"You know, maybe one night you could try staying over here and maybe we wouldn't run into this sort of thing. As part of giving us a try?" she asks.

The reminder is like a punch to the gut. I don't know if I can keep going through with this if I'm developing feelings for Alex. It's not fair to anyone involved.

"It's probably best if we take it slow until we know this is what we want for sure," I say.

"I know it's what I want, Conner. Are you having second thoughts?"

"I can't just make an emotion appear. It takes time. How about lunch tomorrow?" I suggest.

"Conner, we can't just keep doing dates."

"That's how people get to know each other Jand decide if they want to be in relationships. They do things together. What do you want to do?"

"I want to go to bed. I'll call you tomorrow."

The line goes dead. I grab my charger and the turtle and

head for my room. I've got an amazing son who I love, a woman across the hall who is making me feel things I've never felt before and who I shouldn't be attracted to if I'm going to make this work with Jake's mom, and my son's mother who says she wants a family but isn't willing to put in the time. Life is about to get very interesting.

CHAPTER FIVE

Alexis

A few days after my successful interview at the gym, I head behind the counter, clock in, and then just stand there by myself with a smile. I smile at a couple ready for an hour of yoga, rubber mats rolled neatly under their arms. Each of them runs their keys over the corner of the counter until a beeping noise occurs, then continue on their way past me.

Another man and a woman, who look to be the most fit people I've ever seen, walk through the sliding doors a moment later. He slings a bag over his shoulder while she shakes a bottle in her hand. I smile and they both nod in greeting. My hand flies up in an awkward swatting the flies away sort of wave. They don't seem to notice though; they just walk right on by, not doing the weird key thing the couple before them did.

Surely, they've got someone here to train me or at least show me around. Perhaps the lack of attention at the front desk is why they hired me in the first place. I take a step toward the gap that allows people behind the counter, but am distracted by the noise the front door makes when it opens.

Skylar. I haven't seen her since our afternoon hike when I dropped her off here. She must really like the gym.

"Hey Alex," she greets me and her hands immediately go to her hair to smooth is over. When she's closer, I see a smudge of dirt on her face and what I assume is grass in her hair.

"Sleep in the grass lately?" I ask, smiling at my own joke.

She pauses, "Yoga in the park." She shoots me a wink before she scans her card and continues past me.

"Can I help you?" an annoyed voice asks behind me.

I turn, finding the same girl who waited on us at the bar, but who I also didn't officially meet. Abby, I think, is her name. A quick glance at her nametag, which is set in the perfect place to draw attention to her chest, confirms my memory is still all set.

"You're that one girl, aren't you?" Abby continues to glare at me, clearly sounding annoyed with my lack of response.

"If you mean Alex, then yes. I'm that one girl."

Her eyes narrow as her chin rises so she can look me over.

"Sassy one, huh? We might just get along after all."

She taps my shoulder and points behind me.

"First things first, Alex. Greet everyone who walks through the door. Whether it's a smile, a nod, or a simple hello, make sure you acknowledge everyone." She waves to a gray-haired man with a slight limp who has just arrived. "People come here to relax, cool down. Working out is a de-stressor, and people who work out are normally happier too. Don't ruin their workout before it's even begun by pretending you didn't see them."

She's giving me the stink eye again, like I've already done something to not impress her.

"Got it."

"Second, everyone needs to swipe their card. It will beep if their membership is good, and it makes this god-awful buzzing noise if their account is bad."

"Bad?"

"Yeah, like they owe us money because they haven't paid for the month or something."

"And what happens when it buzzes?"

"You tell them they need to pay or leave. It's simple, just don't be a dick about it."

"Okay."

In other words, don't use the tone she has with me right now—check. I don't really have a response to anything she's said so far, but I have to wonder what has happened to give her this attitude with me. Is there some reason she has already decided she doesn't like me? After a moment passes, Abby rolls her eyes before brushing past me toward the other end of the counter.

"We have snacks over here, and this is the list of smoothies and protein shakes we make. I'll teach you those as people order them."

I follow Abby around for a while, nodding my head as she instructs me. She shows me how to make two different smoothies, one from a yogurt machine and one that uses a yogurt powder. Any shake that includes peanut butter is my least favorite and, sadly, they are the most popular. Once I think I've mastered the kitchen part of the job, Abby tells me there is more. Apparently we wash the towels, and, holy crap, this place goes through a lot of them. And in the last hour, one person has come in to sign up. New memberships at this point are not my thing either. Too many numbers to remember.

"Okay, so then we pull all the towels into these giant gray bins and we fold them," Abby says, bringing my attention back to the dang towels.

"All of them?" I ask.

"Yep, and you need to keep up with them throughout your shift, or you will be here after closing, catching up. You don't want to leave work for the person who opens."

"Alrighty."

She tilts her head in annoyance, because, well, I can 90 percent confirm she doesn't like me, at the same time a bald guy in gray shorts and a blue cut-off shirt joins us. He looks young but definitely older than me. The balding is definitely a choice.

"Sorry I'm late. Mrs. Mulligan got to talking about her grandkids again."

Baldy sets his bag under the counter and a grin splits across his face when his eyes land on me. "I'm Pete—you must be Alex. Abby told me you were starting tonight."

I find his comment funny considering Abby pretended she didn't know who I was when she got here. From somewhere next to me, she huffs.

"Back off, Pete, she's with Conner."

"I'm not—"

"You can show her around the back when we get done here. Go shower. You're all sweaty and gross."

Pete chuckles, giving a salute to Abby's back.

I grab a towel and try to mimic her folding skills.

"If you want a player, Conner is definitely a better pick."

I stop folding. A player? Conner?

"Conner's not—"

"Oh, trust me, he is. He's a tease, too, so don't go thinking he's into you if he flirts. That's just who he is. And if you're not looking for a guy, then you might want to keep to the story that you and Conner are a thing or whatever. If you don't, Pete will be all over you."

She hasn't looked at me once, and a part of me wonders if it's possible someone told her the wrong thing about me and Conner, and this could be the reason for her attitude toward me.

"I'm sure you've heard of me. You are hanging out with some people who aren't very fond of me. And I'm sure nothing you've heard is good, but you really shouldn't judge me from what you hear."

"I agree," I say, hoping she catches the hint. By the pause, I'd say she caught on pretty fast.

"Anyway, if you take my advice on anything, it's this: Pete is a cool guy and all, but when he wants something he gets serious fast and it's scary."

"You say that like you've had firsthand experience."

"Just take my word for it." This time she looks me right in the eyes and it makes me cringe. Her eyes mean business. I don't make another comment; instead we fold almost the entire bin, which I'm estimating is at least fifty towels, in silence.

"So are you for real dating Conner Brian? Because I saw him the other night and it didn't look like he was dating anyone," Pete says the moment he's back.

Abby is still folding towels like he isn't even there.

"Sure am," I reply.

Abby makes a choking noise and throws her head back

before returning to her never-ending task. "They're practically living together," she adds.

"Seriously? Well, shit," Pete says with disbelief. "I guess we'd better get to work then. Follow me."

And I do. He teaches me how to pick up weights, clean machines, fill shampoo/ conditioner/body wash and lotion bottles, and take pool temperature. After learning all that, those memberships sound like a fantastic idea. Anything sounds better than having to admit to Conner that I've made him my fake boyfriend. I've known him less than a week. This should go well.

Conner

For the first time in a few days, I find myself with free time that I have no idea what to do with. I've done everything inside my apartment that a guy can do. I've taken out the trash, I've washed sheets and attempted to fold them neatly, I've gone through my junk drawer in the kitchen, and I've made a list of home repair projects I can do on my next day off. Jake is going to love the new shelf I plan to build him. When I ran out of ideas, I even cleaned the bathroom, scrubbed the toilet and all. Now I'm on the couch, bored and not finding anything else to take my mind off my new neighbor or the fact Heather hasn't called me like she said she would and that she isn't answering my calls. I couldn't care less that she hasn't talked to me, but she has my kid so I worry about him. If she's ignoring me ... would she ignore him?

Alex is this breath of fresh air and although I'm really enjoying this upbeat mood that she gave me after hanging out a couple nights ago, I can't help but worry how this is going to affect my relationship with Jake's mom.

I know he and I will be fine, but if Heather knew that I even had the idea of a hanging out with another woman, I'm afraid of how she would lash out at me for it. If she ever tried to take Jake from me, I'd fall apart. That kid is my life. Therefore, I don't feel like sharing any of this information with her just yet. And Alex, she has no idea what's going on between me and Heather. I should probably tell her before it blows up in my face and Alex starts to think for some reason it's her fault I don't want to be with Jake's mom.

I've just leaned back and am about to turn the television on when my cell chimes with an incoming text. It's from Lucas; he wants to head to the gym to shoot some hoops.

I send a quick message back letting him know I can meet him in fifteen minutes. I stuff some clothes into my bag and hop in my truck. The thought that I might run into Alex crosses my mind. I haven't crossed paths with her even once since dinner and I'd be lying if I said I wasn't looking for an excuse to see her again.

With my bag slung over my shoulder and Lucas, who arrives at the same time as I do, doing the same, we head inside. We swipe our cards, and Abby comes out from the small kitchen behind the counter.

"Hey, Conner." She waves at me with a smile that quickly disappears when her eyes find Lucas. She rolls them and walks off.

"What's that about?" I ask.

"Who the heck knows? That girl is pissed at me every other day, I swear it. I wouldn't be surprised if it's over something as dumb as our schedule at the BA. Logan's been giving me Fridays off, and I think it annoys her."

"Why do we all keep hanging out with her?"

"Technically, we all just work together so we aren't actually hanging out," he answers.

"One day I'll have an—"

"Brian! Since when do you have a wicked hot girlfriend and everyone but me knows about it? I swear when the girl told me you two were dating, I didn't believe her."

What's Pete talking about? Shit, is Heather telling people we're an official couple?

"I …"

"Oh, babe! I didn't know you were coming in tonight. I would have been up front, had I known." The odd and fully fake tone Alex uses as she walks up to me is creepy. The moment she wraps her arms around me, we both freeze. I swear, if I didn't know she was pretending, I'd dip my head and place my lips against hers right now. Self-control out the window.

The right side of her mouth tugs into a smile, and she hugs me tighter. I'm definitely going to play along with whatever this it. I give her a squeeze.

"I couldn't wait to see you," I tell her, and it isn't a total lie. It's part of the reason I was so eager to come. Keeping my arms wrapped around her waist, I pull her next to me. She complies easily. Pete just stands there, watching with a doubtful expression on his face, and one quick look at Lucas reveals the exact same expression. He doesn't believe us.

The small shaking from Alex's hand on my hip makes me wonder why she would feel the need to pretend like this. I've heard Pete can come on pretty strong, but I don't remember him being someone you needed protection against.

That's the moment I decide to lean down and kiss the top her head the way I did last night. The moment my lips touch her, she leans into me and I feel as her entire body relax in my arms.

"Alright, well, I'll give you a minute to get whatever display of affection you two need out of your system before we get back to training." Pete pins his stare on Alex. "I'll be up front when you're ready."

He stands there for a good ten more seconds before he glares at me and walks off. I don't think we were as convincing as I wanted us to be.

"Sooo, who is going to explain this to me and can I be there when you explain it to Heather?" Lucas says the moment Pete is out of ears' reach.

Instead of letting go of Alex and answering his question, I keep my hand firmly resting on her hip.

"Can you give us a minute? I'll meet you on the court in about ten minutes."

Lucas leaves without a word, and I'm finally alone with Alexis, and the last thing I want her to do is ask about Heather, so I answer before she gets the chance.

"Heather is Jake's mom."

She only nods.

"I'm so sorry about that, but Abby said he was the type of guy who doesn't stop till he gets what he wants, and then she mentioned how he was looking at me like I was something he wanted, so her suggestion was that since you and I are neighbors, it would be best for me to pretend you are my boyfriend and then I wouldn't have to worry about Pete and—"

"And it sounds like Abby set you up for something."

Her head jerks back slightly as her confused eyes finally make their way back to mine.

"For what?"

I chuckle, shaking my head. "If you can figure out why Abby does half the things she does before the rest of us do, please let me know."

"I think she was being honest."

Poor Alex. She hasn't met the real Abby yet. I resist the urge to pull my hand away, moving it from her waist to rub her arm.

"Why do you think this?"

"Well, she mentioned it as a way to make me feel more comfortable here. If she is a bad as you all say she is, wouldn't she have let Pete pester me?"

She has a point, but it's still a little hard for me to believe that Abby would do a good deed, asking for nothing in return.

"Besides, it doesn't matter. I feel more comfortable doing this, and I'm sorry I just sprung it on you, but can you please play along?"

"This could have been avoided, you know." I'm really only making this comment to put her at ease, because really, I enjoy her hands touching me and claiming me and I hate being worked up about whatever scheme Abby is up to this time.

"How? I didn't know you were going to come in here to work out. I planned to tell you about it when I got home later tonight."

"You could have texted me."

"I don't have your number."

"Yeah, I know. You could have it, though."

"Okay." She pulls out her phone, taps the screen a few times, and thrusts the phone toward me.

"You have to ask," I flash her a grin.

"For your phone number?"

I nod.

"Are you being serious right now?"

Her laugh hits me hard. The sound warms my entire body.

"I never joke when a girl is asking me for my number."

She tries her hardest to keep her lips from cracking a smile but finally gives in.

"Conner, may I please get your—"

"Babe, I told you we could selfie it later, but right now I'll give you what you want till you get home," I cut her off the minute I see Pete walking toward us. I grab her phone, quickly tap the photo button and pull her next to me, my lips gently caress her temple.

It takes a good five seconds for her to figure everything out, then, like before, she does that fake laugh thing that weirds me out as she wraps her arms around me.

"Alright, Brian. You can't come in here and be all over her while she's working."

He's annoyed, but I don't care. He isn't going to touch her now or ever. And after today, that fake laugh is going to be replaced with a real one.

I save the photo we just took and add myself as a contact with the same photo as my profile picture. Then I shoot myself a quick text.

"See you at home," I say with a wink, handing her the phone and heading into the locker room.

As I strip to change into my gym clothes, I send her a message of my own.

. . .

Me: Can I give you a ride home later?

I'm fully changed and about to lock my phone inside my locker when I hear the buzz.

Alex: What makes you think I need a ride?
Me: Your car was at the apartment before I left to come here.
Alex: Creeper, but yes. That would be nice.

I smile, placing my phone in my locker before I step out to join Lucas. I have to tell Heather that being together isn't a good idea. I said I'd try, but it's clear neither of us is going to work hard enough. I can't be with her when this feeling she wants me to have for her is developing for someone else.

CHAPTER SIX

Alexis

It's been a few days since I saw Conner at the gym. Three days I've worked there, and this little voice in the back of my mind hopes he's going to come in. That same little voice is also telling me I should stay clear of him until I come clean to my brother that I'm here. Conner made it clear he isn't a fan of secrets, and I have a one. A big one, too. It may not include him, but it does include someone he clearly cares about. So, yes, there is that. He also asked me, again, via text since I pretended to not be home when he knocked on my door yesterday, to go to this barbeque next weekend and I'm running out of excuses. I told him I had to work, and he said come by after. I said I worked the evening shift, and he said stop by on your way. My only solution now is to completely avoid him until after next weekend.

Between Conner, my new job, the information I've learned since I got here about my brother, and the self-inflicted stress of this secret, my journaling has been in high gear. Today, however, I do not have to work, so instead of writing, I'm going to bake. Since I finally made it to the store, alone I might add, I have everything I need to whip up a fresh batch of chocolate chip cookies.

The dough is made and the first tray is in the oven. I am putting the last measuring cup into the dishwasher when my door opens and in walks Conner. At first I focus on the fact he didn't knock, then I focus on the fact it doesn't bother me and that I'm happy to see him.

"Smells good in here," he says, closing the door behind him.

"Shouldn't you ask permission before you enter an apartment that doesn't belong to you?" I ask playfully. The timer dings and I switch out the baked batch for another one with dough.

"Not when it belongs to my girlfriend."

The oven door slips from my grip and slams shut.

Conner's gaze is drawn to the two pieces of toast with butter and grape jelly spread on them, sitting on a white paper towel in my kitchen. "You're eating that and baking cookies?" he asks.

"Yeah, why not?"

"My old roommate used to eat his toast like that. I honestly never thought I'd meet another person who enjoys it."

"It's good. You should try it, but first let's talk about this girlfriend thing," I joke with him.

"I'm kidding, sort of," he says. "I was at the gym this morning and saw Pete, and I thought to myself, 'We should have a story.'"

"A story?"

"Yeah, like how we met, how long we've been dating, and so on."

"Oh, I don't think anyone is going to interrogate you." I laugh, resetting the timer and moving to the couch. Conner sits next to me, and although he's wearing jeans, the moment his leg touches mine, I'm suddenly very aware that we are alone, again.

"I like to be prepared. What if … we met—"

"In college," I add.

"Ah, no."

"You didn't go to college?"

"Yes and no, why? Does that bother you?"

"Not at all. I didn't go right out of high school. I plan to one day, but not yet."

The right side of his mouth tugs a little as he holds back a smile.

"How about I'm the cousin or sibling of someone you know who he wouldn't know?" It's both a real idea and to test how he would feel about it. Other than Beth, he's the only person I feel comfortable with here so far, so his opinion matters.

"You have the worst ideas ever." He chuckles.

That stings.

"What, how?" I ask, succeeding slightly in hiding my concern over his reply.

His eyes slowly roam over my face.

"Because if you were the sister or cousin of any one of my friends, you'd be off limits. No questions asked. And that is not something I want to think about."

My heart pounds. He just openly admitted that he's attracted to me. He also just told me that if he knew I was

Logan's sister, whatever we have going on wouldn't have a chance. Not in so many words, of course.

"Don't look so panicked. It was a good try, but we can't go with that idea."

The timer dings again, and I spring away from my seat to the kitchen. With a new batch cooling, I begin dropping spoonfuls of dough on to the cookie sheet.

"So, I was thinking." Conner comes up behind me, grabs a cookie, and leans against the counter next to me. He tilts his head, positioning his face closer to mine. My eyes go straight to his lips.

What has gotten into him? Before today, he was a normal hot guy. Now, he's this normal hot guy who is hardcore flirting with me and about to cause my nerves to have a meltdown.

His perfect smile and deep chuckle forces me to blink and realize that I'm staring, and I'm trying to make a giant cookie on the sheet in front of me.

"You want some help?"

"Nope, I've got it."

He nods, his smile growing wider.

"Okay, well, aside from us creating a story, we should go out in public. You know, make it seem more real."

"And do what?"

"Dinner and a movie."

"Like a date?"

"Yes. Exactly like a date."

With the oven timer set once again, I give him my full attention. I swallow, thinking of my answer and praying he can't hear my heartbeat as loudly as I can feel it in my ears.

"Sure. I mean, other than the lake and hiking, I haven't explored much else of this town. We could do that?"

"Great." He grabs two more cookies and heads for the door. "Since you're busy working tomorrow, we can go tonight. I'll pick you up in an hour."

"Sure," I answer again. He flashes me a wink and leaves.

I stand there frozen, staring at the door as if I imagined this entire thing. I'm going on a date with Conner and I have less than an hour to get ready. One hour to shower and get dressed. Not to mention shave my legs, because, let's face it, Conner stirs something inside me that I didn't know was there and I'm not sure I'll be able to resist. That, and I can't wear a dress with hairy legs. I head for the bathroom. I can't waste any time. I want to look good for Conner tonight.

Conner

I've still got it.

I still know how to flirt with a woman. It wasn't easy because nothing with Alex comes easy for me. I mean, seriously, I haven't seen her at the gym and I've been trying to talk to her in person since I gave her a ride home on her first day of work. She's replied to a couple of text messages I've sent her about attending Logan's barbeque with me, but I can't read emotion in a text and it bugs me.

Somehow she managed to make it to the grocery without me. Not that it's a big deal, but I get the feeling she's intentionally trying not to run into me and I have no idea why. Still, I'm not going to let that scare me out of asking her out. Yeah, we had a rocky start, but the night she was over for dinner, I was relaxed. I could just be me and I didn't feel like I had to try hard to impress her. We talked like we've known each other for years, and each time she let out her quirky laugh, I couldn't help but join her. I'm in the mood to feel that way again.

Which is exactly why I made up a reason to go over there. The fresh-baked cookie smell just made me do it sooner.

I jump in the shower and am dried, dressed, and ready in under five minutes. I'm about to call Heather to see if I can get a few minutes of talk time in with Jake when I smell something burning. I glance around my apartment, trying to remember if I shut everything off in the kitchen. The smells gets stronger, urging me to get up and find the problem. As I get closer to the door, it occurs to me that the smell might not be coming from my apartment. Yep, the odor is definitely stronger in the apartment hallway. Opening the door to Alex's apartment without knocking was an afterthought before, but it's completely intentional now. Smoke is coming from her oven. I grab the mitt and open the door, waving the smoke away.

"Alex?" I holler out.

Silence.

"Alex?" I call out again, stepping closer in the direction of her bedroom.

"I'm back here!" she yells back. "I think I broke something."

Letting the oven slam closed, I drop the cookie sheet on the counter and run to her bedroom. Is she okay?

I don't see her, but I hear a grunt from the bathroom. The door is ajar and I push on it gently.

"Hey? Can I come in?"

"Yeah, I don't know what happened."

The door opens fully and I find Alex standing before me in nothing but a towel and head covered in suds. She starts to bend over toward the bathtub, but remembers I'm behind her and jumps back to cover herself. It takes a lot of self-control to not think about the fact that her towel is so small it barely covers her ass cheeks.

"I smelled the cookies and went to get out of the shower and slipped. I grabbed the showerhead but ended up breaking it off the wall, and now when the water is on, it just shoots out all over the place."

"It broke?" Showerheads don't just break off the wall.

"Yep. Mid-shower." She points to her hair and shrugs like she doesn't believe it herself.

"Let me get a look at it while you go across the hall and finish up in my shower."

She nods, sneaking by me. I glance over my shoulder and she looks back. When I shoot her another wink, she blushes and walks away. The moment she's out of sight I rest my hand flat against the wall and release a long, deep breath. She doesn't need to know I freaked out for a second, thinking she was hurt. I never thought my heart could pound so hard with worry for anyone other than Jake. I lean forward and drop my head. And she sure as hell doesn't need to know that my body responded immediately, confirming how much I want her, the moment I saw her in that tiny towel.

When I've got myself together again, sure enough, part of the showerhead is still in the wall and another piece is in the bathtub. On closer inspection, there must be a leak that softened the drywall, probably what made it easy to budge. This building isn't in the best shape, but this definitely needs to be fixed, and someone should have spotted it before they leased the space out again.

I turn the water on, and just as she said, water sprays everywhere, soaking me in the process. Shutting it off, I dry up the mess I made and head back to my apartment to change and send our landlord, Jace, a quick text. I turn the oven off on my way. Baking is not her thing.

The shower is still running as I step into my bedroom to grab a dry shirt. A vision of Alex dropping the towel I just saw her in and letting water glide over her body comes to mind. I freeze. She's naked in my apartment. She's always responded to my flirting—does that mean that if I walked in there, she'd enjoy it as much as I would? Shit, I haven't even kissed the girl, or even planned to kiss her until this very moment, and I'm already jumping to sex in the shower.

I groan so loudly that, if the water weren't running, I'm sure Alex would have heard it. I put on a new shirt and head back out to the living room, receiving a text that says our landlord will be by tonight to look at it. Alex now has something more important to take care of than going to dinner, so I pull out a box of macaroni. Nothing gourmet but still satisfying. The shower shuts off and the door opens a few minutes later, but Alex doesn't come out. After a couple more minutes, I wander down the hall to see what's taking so long.

I find her standing next to my bed, holding up a picture of me, my sister, Sara, and Logan. As much as I love the idea of Alex in a t-shirt and pajama shorts, I clear my throat. She jumps.

"I'm sorry, I thought you were still next door." She blushes.

"Nope, sadly I can't fix your plumbing issue. Jace will be

by tonight. If he can't get it fixed, you can use mine till he does. So I made a plan B for dinner."

"No date?" She frowns.

"We can still have dinner and a movie, just not out. You know, in case Jace needs something."

Alex nods and holds up the photo.

"So how did you become friends with everyone here? School? Or just work?" she asks.

"Yeah, I'm the youngest of the bunch. But it doesn't feel that way. My sister became friends with Sara when they were in grade school, then Sara met Logan. We soon became a group."

"What about your brother-in-law? How did he and your sister get together?"

"Oh, that's a whole other story that you can ask them to tell you someday." I smile—they were on and off more times than a light switch before they finally made it work.

"Alright, well, I guess I'll go finish getting ready, sort of, and be back. I assume you're cooking."

"I sure am."

I walk her to the door and then I cook dinner. The entire night feels like I've done it a million times before. We talk, we laugh, and the next thing I know, it's morning and I'm waking up on the couch with Alex in my arms and a phone that won't stop vibrating against the coffee table. Doing my best to not wake Alex, I pick up my phone and see I've missed three text messages from whom?

Each text is ten minutes apart from the last.

Heather: Meet us for breakfast?

Heather: Hello?

Heather: If you don't want to even try this, I need to know so I can stop wasting my time.

"Everything okay?" Alex asks, catching me off guard. I didn't know she was awake. "You look upset?"

I peel my body away from hers, already regretting it.

"Everything is great. I just forgot about something, is all."

"Okay, well, if you need me to do anything, I'm going to owe you for the next week of showers since Jace said he has to order a part. Let me know."

She winks at me and heads back to her apartment. I stand there smiling like an idiot, thinking of how many more times she going to be naked in my apartment. Then my phone beeps with another text from Heather. Shit, what am I getting myself into?

CHAPTER SEVEN

Conner

It's been a week since I woke up with Alex, and because her shower still isn't fixed, I've had the pleasure of two more nights and mornings just the same. She comes over in the evenings to shower and somehow we end up watching a movie, hardly ever talking, which is both nice and completely odd at the same time, until we eventually fall asleep. Her company is wonderful and everything is great, except one thing: I want to kiss her and I've yet to make that happen. Scratch that, two things: I also haven't decided to stop being a pansy long enough to tell Heather I can't give her what she wants from me.

Until I figure out what I'm going to say to Heather, keeping things uncomplicated between Alex and me is best. Her first impression of me was that I was trying to cheat on Heather, which isn't the case, but I don't know if I would be able to explain it well enough for Alex to understand that.

Shit, I'm about a touch away from just going for it with Alex and taking my chances.

I pull up at Sara and Logan's house, parking my truck on the curb. As usual, Jake has his seat belt off and he's climbing over the backseat to get out on the sidewalk. I walk around to meet him and close the door as he runs to the front yard to play with Clara. Kelsey, Sara, and Beth are gathered in a circle near the front door, each one occasionally stealing at glance to watch over Clara and now Jake.

I grab the potato salad I agreed to bring and walk up to the garage door where Logan, and Ethan are standing.

"What do you think that's about?" I ask both Logan and Ethan, nodding toward the girls.

Logan looks away from the code box on the side of the garage for a brief moment. He shrugs and then goes back to punching in numbers.

"Probably another hormonal thing." Ethan laughs. "You're lucky you aren't living with someone who is pregnant anymore."

"Kelsey wasn't so bad to live with," I say. Logan groans and hits a few more numbers. "Don't you remember the code?"

Logan shoots me a look that says, "Don't ask."

"Besides, you were only the brother, not the husband and father," Ethan says, his eyebrow cocked as he glances between me and Logan.

Logan chuckles and I just shake my head. I'm going to take his word for it.

"Where's Lucas?" I ask. "Isn't he coming?"

I've always hung out with him, but it wasn't until a few months ago he started making plans with Ethan and Logan outside the bar, too. And since he's the only one I've really talked to about Alex, I thought I'd get his opinion, even if I do sound like a girl.

"Someone has to open the bar." Logan laughs.

Like magic, the garage door creaks right before it begins to open. Logan punches his hand in the air with a "whoop" as Sara starts clapping behind us.

"Finally," she says. "Now what's the code before you forget again, telling me I can't use the house key, and we have to go through this another time?"

"I'll tell you later when there aren't so many people around."

Everyone falls silent and we all glare at Logan. For fun, of course.

"Yes, because I can't wait to break into your house. The one that is directly behind my own, where climbing the fence into your backyard would be a lot easier," Kelsey says with humor.

"Babe, climbing fences is not your thing," Ethan says with a chuckle.

Sara then punches Logan on the arm and he fakes an injury before giving in.

"Okay, don't laugh, but it's 0606."

Everyone laughs.

"Wow, I've never been so impressed with my husband," Sara comments as she passes him into the garage on her way to the backyard. Everyone else quickly follows.

"So tell me about this new neighbor of yours. Lucas and Ethan both say I need to meet her ASAP," Logan says, walking directly to the barbeque, opening the lid and holding the ignition switch until a flame appears.

"How did you get that in here if you couldn't remember the code?"

Again, Logan shoots me a look.

"He brought it over the day the inspectors were here," Sara answers as she takes a seat at the patio table. I'm going to assume they also brought that when the inspectors were here. "Once the contractor was done and all we had left was the inspection, they told us we could move some stuff. We just can't sleep here until the house has been approved by the inspector."

If I ever build a house, I'll keep that in mind.

"So back to this girl," Logan brings Alex up once again.

I can't help but smile. It's dead giveaway that I'm into her.

"I invited her today, but she said she had plans."

"I was just at the gym. She wasn't there," Beth says, sitting next to Sara.

"She didn't say what time she had to work," I reply.

"Then what is she doing? She doesn't know very many people in this town. In fact, I'm pretty sure everyone she knows is sitting right here."

"I don't know."

"You should ask these things," Beth says and then starts to text away on her phone like she always does.

"Anyway," Logan says with annoyance. He has this thing about cell phones making people unsocial. "Is she hot? I hear Ethan almost caught you two kissing. I got to say man, it's nice to hear you're into someone again. I didn't want to admit it for fear that was what you wanted, but I don't think Heather is the right woman for you."

"Yeah, me neither. I still haven't figured out how to tell

her either. And yes, of course Alex is hot. But the best part about her is her—"

"You know what, let's not talk about Alex. I remember how defensive you got over her when we went boating the other week," my sister interrupts.

"Yeah, because you were asking her personal questions. Shit, I'm into the girl and I haven't even asked her things like that."

"One, maybe you should. Two, watch your language around the kids. And three, can I have a word with you in private?"

My sister gives me that same glare she used in high school when I would do something to embarrass her and her friends. The "I mean business if you don't do what I say" look. Clara, better watch out. Kelsey has only perfected the look over the years.

I follow Kelsey into the house and into one of the bedrooms. She closes the door and immediately starts in on me.

"What do you know about this girl?"

"Who, Alex?"

"Yes, Alex." She rolls her eyes at me.

"I know enough. Why, what's the big deal?" I never did get a chance to talk to Ethan about his behavior the other day. Asking my sister is basically the same thing. "And explain to me why Ethan was being so weird on the boat."

"Is Alex her full name?"

"I think so, why?"

"What's her last name?"

"I don't know."

"Seriously, you haven't asked her what her last name is?"

"Well the subject has never come up."

"Not even when you introduced yourselves? It's a basic question, Conner. Usually it gets answered on the first date."

"Kelsey, just get to the point," I say, annoyed that she makes a valid argument. *How do I not know her last name?* Whatever is going on with my sister and this mini interrogation she has going on, needs to find an end, quick. The fact that she is questioning Alex pisses me off. Alex doesn't deserve to have people questioning her behind her back when they don't even know her.

"Ethan thinks Alex is Logan's sister, and I think he might be right."

I laugh, but when I catch the blank stare she's still giving me, I refuse to let her continue with her silly accusation.

"Wow, you two have really lost your minds." My voice is deep and firm. "I'm not even going to ask what or how you think this, because it is so freaking crazy. Don't you think she would have told him or someone by now?"

"Some people hide this sort of thing."

"You know, I'm happy Alex had plans. I wouldn't want to put her with a houseful of people who think she's hiding something. She's a normal woman trying to do something different with her life. It's possible some people can start over without keeping secrets."

I head for the door.

"Conner, I'm not saying she's a bad person. I'm just saying maybe you can talk to her about it. If it's true, maybe she needs someone to help her."

"And make it sound like I'm accusing her of something the way you are? I don't think so."

I say goodbye to the rest of the party and head home,

thankful that Jake is having a sleepover with Clara. His dad wouldn't be much fun tonight.

On my drive I receive a text from Logan that reads "If you like this girl, don't let your sister's opinion or anyone else's get in the way. If you *really* like her the way you say you do, this feeling only comes once in your life. Don't let it go."

Such a sappy line from a guy, but he's right. It's time I did something about my feelings for Alex. Now, all I need is for the right moment to make that happen.

I can't remember the last time I had a Saturday night off. A month ago, maybe. It feels like a lot longer than that. A year ago I would have quit my job the first weekend they tried to schedule me. I would be drinking, barely able to stand by midnight, and the girl I'd be planning to take home would be a smidgen more sober than I was. I thought those were the best nights of my life. But tonight, none of that sounds even close to what I want to do. I can't imagine a better evening than one in my quiet apartment. I'll probably do some junk food binging and hang out in a pair of boxers not giving a damn with a beer or two. It'll be stress-free. The perfect way to calm down after that talk with my sister. I don't know what's going on, but she is slowly losing her mind. Alex and Logan, brother and sister. Yeah, there's no way that could be possible.

I switch on the TV then, in nothing but a pair of navy gym shorts, flop down onto the couch and pull out my cell phone to order a pepperoni pizza and one of those chocolate lava dessert things. They're the shit. After I make my order, I lean back into the black leather couch, relaxing at the coolness that touches my skin.

I bet the mailbox has her last name on it. I would need a key to open it to physically look at her mail, so I can't use that route, but maybe she leaves it lying around the apartment. I need to be more observant when I'm at her place next time. Or I could just do what makes the most sense and straight up ask her. Whatever, I need to decide quick because if Kelsey pulls that crap again, I want to be ready.

I'm crossing my feet on the ottoman in front of me when I hear my front door open and close.

Crud. I thought she was working tonight.

The stress-free aspect of the night partially applied to her. Yeah, I want to kiss her and do anything else she lets me, but I haven't fully decided whether or not that's the right move right now. No matter how badly I want her.

Jeez, I don't even know her last name. What else don't I know? I can't be making decisions like this when I'm obviously clueless to certain areas of her life.

Alex steps into view, pausing and starting toward me from the entryway. Her hair falls straight around her face, and those big brown eyes widen when they take in the sight of me on the couch.

We've been living next door to each other for a few weeks, but knowing she's just across the hall from me has forced me to learn a stronger sense of self-control that's bound to break at any moment. Even after it's been brought to my attention I need to know more about her, I still think she looks sexy in everything she does—imagine the amount of seductiveness she holds when she's half naked and on her back.

"Oh, I didn't realize you were here," she says and a shy expression crosses her face. She adjusts the strap of her bag over her shoulder. "I was just going to take a quick shower. I won't bother you." She turns quickly, heading down the hall. And now she's going to be naked again in my apartment. Awesome. It's been easy to resist her when I've been at work while she's showering or Jake is around, but right now the temptation is much higher.

"I just ordered pizza," I say. I keep thinking I'm going to say something smart or funny to catch her attention, but lately, every time I talk to her, it's normal and boring. And I never say enough to keep her talking. I put my feet down and sit up straight, muting the TV. "There's enough for two, if you want some."

"I don't want to ruin your evening, Conner. I've been here almost every night this week. I'm sure you want some time to yourself."

"You won't ruin anything," I say, too quickly.

A shy smile touches her lips, but she nods. "Okay, I'll be quick." She continues down the hall and when I hear the door lock, I release a long breath.

Self-control, if you're there, now is the time to come out.

A whole night in, just the two of us. This isn't the first time. I shouldn't be nervous, but Logan's text is flashing in my mind and tonight is going to be different. I know I want her. I know I want her more than anyone else I've ever met. I don't want to screw this up. Shit, we haven't even started anything and I'm worried about messing it up.

I groan, rubbing my hands down my face. The knowledge that she's taking her clothes off right now is killing me. I can't imagine what an entire night alone is going to do to me. I've never acted like this. Naked women aren't rare. I could go to any bar, find one, and bring her home. The only downfall is my body doesn't want that. It wants the sexy blonde with legs, the one who's always around but completely untouchable. Until now. *Why does this girl have me so thrown off?*

Fifteen minutes later the bathroom door opens, hinting that she's coming out, and I readjust myself on the couch. I've been sitting in the middle and decide my best option right now is to choose a side. I'm half sitting when I glance up to see legs. Long, tan legs in a pair of light purple shorts that stop just under her butt cheek. She's wearing a gray tank top with a silver heart over the chest and *Lord help me*, she's not wearing a bra. All the other nights she was *always* wearing a bra.

Her perky breasts are hidden behind the design, but I've seen enough in my day to know the way a set of free tits sit. And Alex's are the best ones I've ever set my eyes on.

As if she could feel me watching, Alex crosses her arms and a light pink flushes across her face. I finish taking my seat, clear my throat, and wish myself luck.

"Jammie night, huh?" I say, cringing immediately.

Jammie night? *What the fuck, Conner?*

A giggle erupts from her throat, and I'm immediately turned on. I need to get control of myself now, or this entire night is going to be a disaster. Little noises like that shouldn't excite me.

"Yeah, it looks that way," she says, taking a seat next to me. "Where's Jake? Wasn't he here earlier?'

"Yeah, he's spending the night with my sister."

"That's cute."

I nod.

"So what are you watching tonight?" she asks.

I turn the volume back on and smile. "*Jurassic Park.*"

"Which one?"

"The first one."

"The first is the best one," she says, tucking her legs underneath her. Her knees fall to the side and miss brushing against my arm by less than an inch. One advantage of owning two loveseats is the closeness we have right now. The disadvantage? I could touch her with just a twitch of my pinky finger, and I really, *really* want to touch her.

I lick my lips and return my focus to the TV. The man on the shitter is getting eaten by the T-rex. Yes, this is good. Totally not sex related. Now the kids are screaming. Perfect, this is a great distraction.

Alex gasps when the car is knocked over the ledge. All that hard-earned focus is gone.

"I was under the impression you've seen this movie," I say, observing the look on her face. She doesn't look startled or worried. She looks … nervous.

"I have." Her eyes focus on mine. I have to look away from the heat that comes from them. "But seriously, being attacked by a meat-eating dinosaur will never get easier."

My gaze is back on the TV before I say, "We can watch something else if you want."

"No, I want to watch this." She sits up, letting her legs fall to the other side. She leans back, and on instinct, I reach my arm around as she rests against my side, nestled next to my side. Her body freezes and so does mine. All the other nights that happened somehow after we'd fallen asleep. We are definitely awake and aware this time around.

A lustful look fills her eyes as she leans her head back, looking up at me. I start counting. One, I shouldn't kiss her.

She could be a convicted and wanted felon for all I know and I've been reading about her in the paper but would never know because I don't even know her whole name. Two, this is a bad idea. I should keep her as my neighbor and my friend. Jake likes her—I can't ruin that. Three, but she smells like peaches. Four, if I can't even tell her what's going with Jake's mom, crossing the friendship line is the last thing we should do. Five, *fuck it.* I lean down and her eyes close. I feel her breath against my lips.

Knock, knock.

Alex jumps and I back away as though we've been caught. The knocking on the door starts again, and I'm not happy about it the way normal people would be.

For once, the pizza has arrived on time and ruined everything.

Alexis

Deep breaths. It's fine. I'm fine. He's fine. *Oh boy, is he fine.*

Conner being home totally threw me off when I came here to shower. He said he was going to a barbeque at Logan's house. What's he doing home so early? And please don't ask why I'm not at work.

"Do you want any kind of dipping sauce? Like ranch or something?" Conner pokes his head around the wall that separates his kitchen and living room.

"Do you have Dorothy Lynch?" I ask. I know it's totally gross, but it tastes so good. It's like cinnamon rolls and chili. Sounds terrible but absolutely freaking delicious. His eyes narrow as he stares at me. He nods slowly but doesn't say anything before bringing out two plates, Dorothy Lynch dipping sauce included.

"Did your plans for tonight get canceled?" he asks.

Damn.

"Um, no. I actually was just planning to get a little reading or writing in tonight."

"I was turned down because a woman wants to read or write more than she wants to hang out with me, huh?" He takes a bite of his pizza and gives me a closed-mouth smile.

"Well, when you say it like that, it sounds bad."

Really, Alex, you couldn't come up with a better answer?

"It's actually kind of hot. I like a woman who is into more than texting or watching TV or drama. What I know about you now tells me you aren't like those kind of girls."

"Yeah, I guess we don't really know that much about each other." I laugh because it is weird I like to hang out with him but really only know he has a kid, works at a bar, is friends with my brother, enjoys running shirtless, plays basketball at the gym, may or may not be a college student, and … wait, I know a lot more than I thought I did.

"We could play twenty questions," he says with an eagerness that raises a red flag. There might be something particular he wants to ask me. Does he know who I am?

"Maybe another night," I say in my flirtiest tone and then I shove a piece of pizza into my mouth as I focus on the TV. I hear his deep chuckle, but he doesn't say anything.

We continue watching the movie and eating in silence. Conner gets up for a second round and I watch his body move in its shirtless and hairless glory. I have no idea how I lucked out on moving in next door to such a sexy man. I mean, up until tonight, I wasn't completely sure he was attracted to me.

Yeah, he's flirted and we've hung out, but after the fifth or sixth time, I was sure the flirting would upgrade to a kiss by now. It never happened.

And then tonight … well, I hope he won't think I'm too desperate if I try to get us back there. I mean, just looking at him makes me want to climb on top of him and kiss him till he blacks out. I want to touch the rippled muscles I've see him create in the gym. Is that too much to ask? It's when I remember how much of a chicken I am—my making the first move is highly unlikely—that I relax a little. Then again, if we are kissing, we can't be talking and that's a good plan for me.

"Are you okay?"

Conner's voice startles me, and I quickly take in the fact that he's already sitting back down and halfway through another piece of pizza. Oh, and I'm staring right at his chest.

"Yep," I say, forcing a smile as I look back to the TV. I may as well stand up and shout "kiss me" already. My eyes basically did it for me.

He sets his plate on the coffee table and then, as if it were the most normal thing in the world, he scoots over till he is right next to me and places me right back under his arm. I relax into him and do nothing to stop the huge smile on my face.

"I don't care how this sounds, but I'm not letting you leave here tonight without getting the chance to taste your lips at least once."

I swallow, allowing his words to sink in right before I press my lips against his. He kisses me back, the pressure soft and gentle, as though he wants to make it last. Everything inside me warms as the arms around my shoulders squeeze me tightly. I begin to shift, to deepen the kiss when Conner pulls away.

He releases a breath I hadn't noticed he was holding and tugs my body closer to his. Once I'm snuggled in next to him on the couch, he kisses me again. This time it's more urgent. His tongue parts our lips and finds my own as our mouths move more quickly against each other. My eyes close as I absorb the way kissing Conner feels. Sweet, scary, right, and like I never want him to stop.

In seconds, Conner rolls his body on top of mine. His knee nudges itself between my legs as he breaks the kiss to press his lips to my jaw, my neck, my collarbone. I use this time to take a deep breath, because I plan on kissing him as long as I can. A wave of his woodsy scent fills the air and fuels something inside me. I pull his face back to mine.

Hours pass as we make out like teenagers on his couch. I love it though, and I love it even more when I wake up the next morning still tucked under his arm on the couch. The thought that it's time I tell him who I am ruins the entire moment for me. But I have to tell him. Whatever we've started I want it, and it'll only work if he knows the truth. All I have to do is figure out how I'm going to tell him.

If only it could be that simple.

CHAPTER EIGHT

Conner

There's a good chance I've been making out with my best friend's little sister for the last week. A really good chance, but I'm not ready to accept it or question her yet. Although it drives my mind wild wanting to know more, or simply her freaking last name, we're in a good place and I don't want to ruin it if I'm wrong.

Beth unlocks the door, signaling that it's time to open The Black Alcove. I have a whole night's worth of work before I'll see Alex again, and it's killing me. I want to see her because I'm into her, of course, but also because now that my sister brought it to my attention, I notice little things that are making me think maybe Alex really is Logan's sister. First it was the way she looked around my living room that day, then it was the butter and jelly toast thing, and then when she wanted Dorothy Lynch for her pizza dipping sauce. I know it sounds crazy, but those are all things Logan likes—it could be a family thing.

"What's got you so focused?" Beth pulls up a seat at the bar across from where I'm standing. She's on the clock, but with zero customers right now, she doesn't have anything else to do.

"It's nothing."

"I've known you for years, Conner, so I know when something is bothering you."

Beth looks me in the eye, and it occurs to me that she, being the bluntest woman I know, would have called me out on the Alex thing if she knew what my sister or Ethan thought. There's a good chance she doesn't know about the hunch, so I could get advice from her.

"Alright, so you know I've been hanging out with Alex?"

"Yes, I do."

"I want to get to know her more, learn about her past, but I don't know how to bring it up."

"That's easy."

I knew asking her was a good idea.

"You don't bring it up," she finishes and I frown.

"What?"

"That girl came here for a reason. I don't know what it is, but it's clearly to either get away from something or to find something, and a new guy in her life bringing up her past isn't going to help her get anywhere positive," Beth says the words as though they mean something to her or as if she is talking about herself. I'm about to ask more on the subject when Heather comes storming into the bar, Jake following closely behind her. The first thing I notice is how she almost hit him with the door when she didn't hold it for him, and then I notice the tears running down her face.

"Conner, something came up and I need you to take Jake for a few nights."

"Dad!" Jake cheers when he sees me.

Beth excuses herself but doesn't go far as I walk around the bar to meet them near the door.

"What's going on?" I ask.

"Nothing that concerns you or Jake. He just needs to stay with you for a few days."

She shoves a full backpack against my chest and turns for the door.

"Heather, I'm working. I can't just leave right now."

"So let him stay here. I don't care."

"This is a bar!" I catch the rise in my voice and glance to Jake. His eyes are wide and on the verge of tears. I crouch down and hug him. I stand again, with Jake in my arms, and keep my voice calm.

"Heather, this isn't the place for a kid to be hanging out all night."

All she does is shrug and walk out the door.

I set Jake on his feet and he runs over to Beth, who's holding a tray with a bowl of ice cream and toppings. She sets the tray on the bar top as Jake climbs onto a stool and begins dumping sprinkles over the bowl.

He can't stay here, but whatever his mom has going on, anywhere is better than with her right now.

Scratching the back of my head, hoping the movement will send an idea to mind, I head for Jake and Beth, who is now sitting with my son. My parents and my sister are the obvious choices for babysitting duty.

"Everything okay?" Beth asks.

I pull out my phone and start to dial my sister.

"It will be."

"Hey guys." Alex's bright smile catches my attention from across the bar, and I pause before I hit the call button. She looks amazing as her dark red corduroy skirt sways from side to side with each step, revealing her legs. "Hey, Jake, do you remember me?" Her face lights up at the sight of him, and I know mine mimics that expression at her excitement to see my son. He nods quickly but is more focused on his bowl of ice cream.

"What are you doing here?" she asks, eyeing me for the answer.

"Mom said I was staying with my dad for the week," he says between bites and not looking at her.

This *week*? I thought she just said a few days. I work four out of five nights.

"That's so awesome." Alex's happiness momentarily distracts me.

"What are you doing tonight, Alex?" Beth asks.

"Nothing. I have the night off so I thought I'd come in here and maybe grab some dinner."

"Jake, you want to eat dinner with Alex?" Beth asks my son, and I start to put the pieces together. Beth is a good friend to think of it, but this isn't something I'd ask Alex to do.

Jake looks at me, waiting for me to answer for him, and when I give him a smile, he nods.

"I'll go get something started for you both."

Beth moves to the back, sending me a look on her way. She wants me to ask Alex to watch Jake. The only time they met was the day she moved in, and even though Jake is acting like he remembers her, he could be doing that only because I'm here. He could be different when they're alone. I can't just ask the girl I'm trying to date to watch my son. She'll probably say yes because she feels obligated, and I don't want to put her in that situation.

Alex is leaning over the bar. I really want to kiss her, but I can't do it in front of Jake. Not yet.

"You look nice today," I say, setting my phone down and leaning forward on my arms to talk to her.

"Thank you." She blushes, but her smile doesn't falter. "How is it that you're working and Jake is staying with you at the same time?"

I sigh. I shouldn't keep anything else about Jake's mother and myself from her.

"Heather just dropped him off. I had no idea she was bringing him."

"When does your shift end?"

"Midnight, if it's slow," I tell her.

She nods and I can see in her eyes that's she's thinking the same thing as Beth.

"I can't let you do that," I say, cutting the idea off.

"Why not? He'll be at home. It's not like I'm going out of my way and I want to, Conner."

"You want to hang out with my four-year-old son?"

"Yes, I do."

"I don't know …"

"I can handle it, I promise. I grew up in a house with tons of kids younger than me. I know what to do."

A foster house, or brothers and sisters?

"Do you have a lot of brother and sisters?" I ask, taking the safe road.

"No" is her only answer before she gives her attention to Jake.

A few customers come in and I help them while Beth brings out a burger for Alex and chicken fingers for Jake. Somewhere in the next hour, I gave her my permission to watch Jake. Of course, it was after I texted Lucas, who said he could come in and relieve me of my shift around eight thirty.

I trust Alex, and I trust that Jake will be good for her. It's only for a few hours. I just don't want her to think that our being together means she needs to be responsible for him. Becoming an instant parent can freak a person out. I know from firsthand experience how stressful it can be. I'd never pick Alex over Jake, but being with her gives me hope that I can give Jake everything. I don't want anything to ruin that. When Heather picks Jake up, I'm telling her it's not going to work.

Alexis

Never did I think I would be that girl, the one who's awkward with children. Growing up, everyone liked me. I was a fun person so be around. But now, hanging out with Jake is different. I never really cared if the other kids liked me, but this one … I want him to like me. And now that we're alone without Conner, things are a bit … awkward.

I thought watching Jake in Conner's apartment would be best, but right now, I don't think it would have mattered.

Jake is sitting on the couch across from me with his arms crossed and the best scowl a four-year-old can give. He crosses his ankles and his eyes narrows. He looks just like his father.

Except this kid gives some seriously good dirty looks, where Conner's never look like he's mean mugging me.

His eyes shift with every move I make. He isn't going to let me out of his sight.

"So," I say, trying my hardest to let my expression give away the fact he's making me a bit nervous, but this kid's hard stare is about to make me crack. "What do you like to do for fun besides play basketball with your uncle and dad?"

He doesn't say anything. He just keeps staring.

"Do you like to watch movies?"

I wait for him to respond or maybe even shake his head. I get nothing. This kid talks all the time. What has gotten into him?

"What about dinosaurs?"

I wait.

"Turtles?"

His eyes narrow less, but it's something. Okay, it's possible he likes turtles.

"Do you like the Ninja Turtles?"

His chin raises, and for a split second I think he's going to speak, but then he quickly returns to his scowling state.

Damn.

What did I like as a kid? Who am I kidding—I hardly had any of my own toys and this kid has a room with all of his.

Think, *think*. Build a tent. No. Pretend the remote is a car? No. Oh, yes! I got it.

I jump onto my seat, my feet landing in the center on the small couch.

"Did you see that?" I ask, sounding amazed. "The lava, it boiled. Right there, right there by your foot."

Jake peeks his small head over the edge of the couch. When he catches sight of the carpet, he looks at me, confused.

"Look! You missed it. I did it again."

His head flashes back toward the ground. He stares for a minute before slowly reaching his hand over the couch.

"Don't touch it," I say, faking a panic. "It will burn you."

His hand jerks back and he moves fast to stand on his couch cushion as well. A small smile starts to touch his lips as he watches me.

I jump to his same cushion.

"Don't let your feet touch the floor or the lava will burn them," I whisper. His eyes widen with excitement as he steps cautiously to the end of the sofa. He gently steps onto the end table next to him.

"Careful," I say, both referring to the game we're playing and to the fact I'm totally allowing this kid to climb on the furniture when I know I shouldn't be.

Once both of his feet are planted on the table, he looks over at me with a huge smile. Quickly we move from couch to chair to table and back to the couch. Every now and then I pretend I'm about to fall, and once Jake even reached out to help me. He still hasn't spoken, but from the joy written on his face and the loud giggles coming from his tiny body, I know I'm getting closer.

I'm on my hands and knees now, crawling across the sofa.

"Stop," he says and I freeze. He places his small finger in front of his lips. "It can hear you."

I fake the best scared face I can as I lean over the sofa to hide the smile that snuck out at the fact he talked. Finally. My eyes go wide as I get ready to pretend I fall in again. Jake's serious face is back. My hand reaches closer to the carpet. He leans forward just a little.

"Fuck!" Conner yells as the front door slams against the wall.

A scream passes Jake's lips as he leaps onto the chair. For real this time, I fall off the couch.

"What are you guys doing in here?" Conner asks as he steps into the living room. Jake scurries across the floor to where I fell.

"You made her fall."

"You fell?" Conner rushes to me and helps me up.

"I didn't fall, fall," I say, glancing to the clock.

"Yes, you fell into the lava!" Jake shouts.

"The lava?" Conner asks.

"Yeah, we was playing a lava game, and we had to jump on the couch!"

I give my best smile as Conner glances at me with one eyebrow raised.

I just shrug.

"It happens, but more importantly, why are you storming into your apartment shouting profanities, and how are you off when I left you an hour ago?"

Conner's eyes capture me where I stand. He never lets the connection break, not even as a grin appears on his lips. He takes a deep breath and I do the same. He tucks a loose strand of hair behind my ear, his hand lingering. The urge to tilt my head slightly comes to me, to let it rest in his hand.

"Just a scheduling conflict that is long forgotten now that I'm home with the two of you, and Lucas was able to come in sooner. That guy is a workaholic."

"Fuck," Jake's little voice says from somewhere around us.

Conner groans and I cover my smile with my hand. "You need to start watching your language. You know he repeats everything you say."

"Yeah, I know." His head drops and his hands go to his hips. "Hey, bud, what did I say about that word?"

"No."

"Right, so why did you say it?" Conner asks, stepping up behind Jake at the table. In the time it took for Conner and me to stare at each other, Jake's little attention span has forgotten all about the lava game and he's already moved on to coloring at the table.

"My blue crayon broke," he answers.

"Aw, that's no fun. Let me see if I can find you another one," Conner says, stepping over the rectangle Tupperware box full of crayons. We both sit with him at the table then, coloring for about a half hour before it's time for Jake to get ready for bed.

Once he's all tucked in, Conner comes down the hallway to find me in the living room. I've put in a movie and am sitting on the couch, hoping he doesn't want me to leave quite yet. And I am right. He takes the seat next to me before kissing me and guiding me onto my back. I was going to tell him about me and Logan tonight, but this is a much, much better idea.

CHAPTER NINE

Conner

Alex steps out of the bathroom with wet hair, fully dressed in her work shirt.

"Not that I mind," I say from the living room. "But has Jace told you when he's going to have your shower fixed?"

"All he keeps saying is, 'I'm waiting on a part,' and since I know nothing about plumbing, I have no reason not to believe him."

"You could call someone else. Have them come look at it."

"Yeah, but then I'd have to pay for it myself, and I'd miss out on all these awesome moments of being in your apartment."

"Eh," I joke with her.

She shoves me as she takes a seat next to me on the couch, kissing me in the process.

"What time do you have to work today?" I ask her.

"Eleven to five."

"Would you be interested in joining Jake and me in the park tonight for a picnic dinner?"

"Just the three of us?" she asks as though she's worried it won't be.

"Yes." Her eyes flutter around the apartment the exact way Logan's do when he doesn't know what to say. She's done this before, and I never thought anything of it. Now, all I can think about is what Kelsey mentioned to me. I just need to come right out and ask Alex before I let it bother me much more.

"Please, Miss Alex. It will be so fun. They have swings and slides," Jake says as he pokes his head out of his room. The two of them have been interacting a lot. The fact that Jake enjoys her company as much I do makes the idea of talking to Heather sound so simple.

"Is your bed made?" I ask. He isn't supposed to come out till his room is clean. It's something else he seems to be having a hard time with. My sister says getting him to clean his room at this age is tough and I might have to wait another year or two till it clicks, but my kid is smart and I think he'll catch on sooner than she thinks.

He nods.

"And your toys are in their buckets?"

He puckers his lips and then disappears back in his room.

"Did he do something wrong?" Alex asks.

"No, why do you ask?"

"I always had to clean my room extra good when I was in trouble. It looked a little like what I just saw."

Perfect opening line to ask her more, ignoring Beth's advice completely.

"Done!" Jake hollers as he runs out of his room,

preventing me from asking the question on my lips. *Are you Logan's sister?*

Jake plops his small body between Alex's and my own.

"Can we bring cookies to the park?" he asks. I find it weird that he's looking at me and not Alex.

"Shouldn't you be asking me that question?" she says, gaining his attention.

He shrugs. "I don't like burnt cookies."

Alex erupts into laughter as she stands and grabs her stuff.

"Once, I did that once," she says as I follow her to the door. "I can't believe you told him about that."

"I'll pick you up?" I ask, grinning at her playful tone.

"Sounds great."

I kiss her goodbye and then head back into the living room where I proceed to play Ninja Turtles with my son, he as Donny and me as Shredder until it's time to pack up a picnic and pick up Alex from work. I try to call Heather twice to see if whatever was going on a couple days ago is better today, and also because I don't want to wait any longer to tell her about Alex, but just like the last two nights, she doesn't answer any of my calls.

Four other cars fill the parking lot aside from mine as I head inside the gym. Must be a slow afternoon. Jake runs inside in front of me, slowing to let the automatic doors open for him.

Abby is standing behind the counter when we walk in. Her face breaks into a smile when she notices me, and I feel like a dick immediately because it's the same type of smile Alex gives me. I know what that smile means, and even though I shouldn't, I feel guilty that I don't return those feelings for Abby.

"Well, this is a surprise. What brings in the two of you?" She stops folding the towel in her hands to give me her full attention. Pete walks up in the same moment.

"What, she can't even work one day without you showing up?" he asks. I can't tell by the tone of his voice if he's annoyed or really bad at joking. It's like a mix of sarcasm and light bitterness. We may have told him we were a couple before it was really true, but at least now we don't need to pretend.

"I can, but yeah, I'm actually here to pick up Alex."

Abby's smile drops and she turns, resuming her task.

"You mean *Alexis*." She mumbles the name in a sassy tone, but I caught it loud and clear. Maybe I was listening for it, or maybe it's just what I was hoping to hear.

"Did you say Al—"

"Did you say my name?" Alex comes from the back room, where I know they keep the washing machines. She stops and gives me a beaming smile. "I'm almost done. Give me ten more minutes to finish picking up the weight room and I'll meet you two outside."

"I'll help you," Pete says, grinning at me as he strides past her.

I nod, say goodbye to Abby, and then convince Jake it's better to let her finish than to bother her when he wants to run back to the basketball court before we return to the car. If I see him hitting on her or even standing too close, I'll probably end up punching the guy.

When Alex comes out, she's followed by Abby and the girl I saw her on the trails with. Skylar, I think was her name.

Pete is nowhere to be found, and I breathe a sigh of relief. I've never been a jealous guy and I have to say I don't like it. The best thing I can do here is to not even bring it up. This is still new.

Abby quickly walks away toward her car, and then Skyler waves as she backs away and sets off in the other direction. Alex doesn't move for a moment before she heads for my truck.

"Is everything okay?" I ask as she buckles her seat belt.

"Yes. Abby is just being weird." She sighs. "She was fine up until we left, and then it was like I was her least favorite person ever."

I glance back to find Jake focused on his LeapPad.

"I may actually be the one to blame for that," I say, backing out of the parking lot.

"Why?"

"Last year, Abby stayed with me and my buddy Logan for a while when she didn't have a place to go. Somewhere during that time, she thought something was going to happen between the two of us. It wasn't. Ever. But now I think she is taking the fact I'm not into her out on you."

All I get is a blank stare. "Girls suck sometimes," she says.

I agree and pull onto the road. Skylar is walking alone toward the center of town.

"Does she walk everywhere?" I ask.

"You know, I'm not quite sure.

"I thought you two were friends."

"We are."

"Do you think she needs a ride?"

"Really? I bet she'd love that. Slow down, I'll ask her."

I slow the truck as instructed and Alex rolls down her window. I catch a glimpse of Jake stretching his neck to look out the window.

"Hey, Skylar, do you need a ride?" Alex asks.

"No thanks." Skylar stops walking only long enough to answer.

"Are you sure?"

"Yeah, I'm just going to the diner across from the BA. I work the evening shift tonight."

"I didn't know you worked there."

"It's not really something I brag about."

I pinch Alex's side to get her attention. She jumps at my touch and then laughs, turning to face me.

"Tell her to come to the BA—it's better money and I know she'll get hired."

"Conner says you should go to the BA. He might be able to set you up with a better paying job."

"Seriously?" Skylar's face lights up. "I don't know anything about making drinks, though."

"He can teach you," Alex answers for me.

"Okay, I will." She waves. "See you both later."

Alex rolls up her window and gazes at me with a smile.

"You're turning out to be one of those extremely rare types, aren't you?"

"What do you mean?"

"The guy who can do no wrong. Completely trustworthy and dependable," she says.

"Maybe, that depends."

"On what?"

"Are you into that sort of guy?"

"Yes. One hundred percent."

I reach over and lace her fingers through mine as we head for the park.

"It's always about the percentages with you, isn't it?"

She laughs but nods.

"Before I forget, this weekend a friend of mine is having a get together. It'd be cool if you can make it."

"Yeah, sure, I'll think about it."

A spark runs through my veins at the idea that she might possibly go out with me. She always has an excuse—or really does have something going on—and the idea that I can finally introduce everyone to her thrills me. Right now might not be the best time to include that the gathering is at Logan's house. If I mention it, it might spook her and then ruin the evening I have planned. But if I mention it and she doesn't react, then I'll know. I just don't want to take that chance with Jake in the car.

Either that, or I'm not ready to face the truth, no matter how much I think about it.

Alexis

An evening picnic is exactly what I need. Ever since I left the gym, I've had the way Abby called me out right before we left work on my mind. She asked if Conner knew my first and last name. She was a snot about it because she's seen the paperwork. But what stumps me is, if she knows, why hasn't she told anyone? If she really is as evil as people say, she would have told someone by now, right?

Once we arrive at the park, we eat peanut butter and jelly sandwiches and then Jake runs off to play. Conner and I take a seat together on the blanket to watch him. Well, mostly

Conner is watching him; my brain is all over the place. Conner kisses my shoulder and hugs me tighter from behind.

"Is everything okay? You seem distracted," he says.

I sigh. This is the perfect moment to tell him. Blurt it out and I'll no longer be keeping a secret from him. "Your best friend is my brother and I need help finding a way to tell him without him rejecting me" are the words resting on the tip of my tongue. If I could just leave it at that and not have Conner ask anything else, I'd be fine. I really don't want to go into the details that I went through four different homes before someone kept me. I don't think I can handle being rejected by anyone else in my life.

"I'm fine. Just thinking about what Jake and I are going to do while you're working tomorrow night," I say instead.

"Oh, he has plenty of toys to keep you busy."

"I bet."

"Dad, I'm bored. Can we go now? Or can Clara come play?"

"It's getting too late for Clara to come play tonight, bud. I'll see what I can do about later this week though, okay?"

"Okay," Jake says with a sad voice.

"How about we go home and you can pick out the movie?" Conner asks.

"Ninja Turtles!" Jake cheers, and we all head for the truck.

"I had no idea he was going to pick out that one," Conner says sarcastically.

I laugh, not caring at all which movie we watch. My mind is still on Abby and what she may or may not do, and on Conner and what I need to tell him but can't seem to find the words.

Conner gets Jake ready for bed and ready for the movie,

but the little guy passes out before the previews are over. When Conner returns to the living room after putting him to bed and takes his seat next to me on the couch, the look in his eyes tells me we won't be watching a movie. The way his lips kiss me make my body feel as though I've been zapped by an electric current.

Conner's lips nip and suck against my neck, and I know there's no way I'm going to be able to stop him. Not tonight. I don't want to stop. That would just be cruel to the both of us. The familiar woodsy scent that consumes me every day surrounds me now, and I finally respond to the bliss he's beginning to put me in. My desire for him becomes uncontrollable.

My hand finds his back, clawing and gripping the best I can. His mouth is working so quickly over me, I need to hold on to him. Make sure his body doesn't move too far away. Make sure my touch can do to him what he's doing to me.

"Alex you're positive this is what you want?" he asks, attempting to pull back, but I don't let him.

I slam my mouth against his, slipping my tongue into his inviting mouth, and I moan, long and deep before pulling away. "I've never wanted someone so bad in my life."

A glimmer in his eyes flashes in front of me before his lips consume mine once again. His hand glides up the side of my thigh, inching the hem of my dress higher and higher until it rests fully around my waist. He grinds his hips into me once before giving enough distance between us to replace his strained jeans with his hand. Moving my panties to the side, he slides two fingers inside my core. My hips buck and my back arches at the feeling—foreplay is usually one of my favorite things, but with Conner, it's too much. I want him. I want him right now, and I can't wait for him to finish whatever he planned. I sit up, his fingers remaining fast at work inside me, and I reach for his jeans. I have his belt and zipper undone and am sliding them off before he lets out a second moan.

With our clothes removed, Conner grabs his pants and pulls a condom from his wallet.

"Shit, we should move this to the bedroom," he says. "Don't think for one second I don't want you, but I don't want to make it easy for Jake to walk out and see this."

I slap a hand to my mouth. "I never even thought of that."

Conner lifts his body off me and I leap from the couch, making a dash for his room.

Naked. I barely make it two steps past him before his arm snakes around my body, capturing me long enough to press me up against the wall, his erection digging into my stomach.

I want you, too.

He begins to kiss my neck, my collarbone, moving farther down at a snail's pace.

"We're not to the room yet," I manage to say. I'd rather not be talking, but the hallway is just as bad as the couch.

"I couldn't let your bare ass run past me without touching you." His lips push against mine and I lock my arms around his neck as he lifts me to wrap my legs at his sides. His steps are quick as he enters his bedroom, but our frenzied lips never part.

Holding tightly, he lowers us to the bed. He breaks the kiss and I look down to see he still has a hold on the gold wrapper. He glides the condom on and positions himself at my entrance.

He pauses, his eyes finding mine, and he smiles. It's contagious. I kiss him then, giving him the go ahead.

He presses inside me slowly, allowing me to savor the moment we're fully connected. He pulls back just as calmly before slamming into me.

"Oh!" I call out. He repeats the action once again, this time covering my mouth to muffle the noises I'm making. I smile under his hand, my eyes locked on his. I lift my hips for him to continue and he takes the hint. He pulls his hand away and covers my mouth with his own instead.

Our kisses become as desperate as every thrust he makes. His pace quickens and right when I feel an explosion ready to ignite, he pulls out and flips me onto my stomach. He's inside me once again before I have time to object.

"Fuck, Alex," he whispers into my ear as his smooth hard abs rub against my back. "You feel so fucking good."

My mind is still processing a response when everything goes black and I let out a moan I've never made before. Conner's body collapses onto mine, releasing a noise similar to my own. He rolls to his side, yanking me back to snuggle against him. Light kisses pepper across my back and that's the last thing I remember before sleep takes over.

I wake the next morning alone and on the couch. I'm wearing a pair of Conner's sweatpants that are struggling to stay around my waist and a t-shirt that hangs almost to my knees. There is also a very awake and observant Jake sitting on the floor in front of the couch, watching me as he eats his bowl of cereal.

"Good morning," I say, keeping myself wrapped in the blanket that lays over me even though I have some of Conner's clothes on.

"Did you spend the whole night at Dad's?" he asks, his mouth full of what I'm assuming from its colorful state is Fruit Loops.

Where is Conner? How do I answer this?

"I must have passed out on the couch after watching a movie," I answer. *What kind of sleep was I in to not notice being moved?*

"That's why Dad says I can't ever stay up late to watch movies. Cuz I'll sleep."

"He's right, and I should have gone to bed instead of staying up."

"Do you live here now?"

"I ... I ..."

"Eggs are ready!" Conner cuts in on the conversation from the kitchen. A full smile lets me know he was listening in the entire time.

"I also made bacon and some toast. Thought you might like food *food* instead of just a bowl of cereal today."

"It smells fantastic." I say, taking notice of the coffee smell that also fills the air.

The moment I step into the kitchen and am out of sight from Jake, Conner wraps his arms around my hips and pulls me in for a kiss.

"How'd you sleep?" he asks.

"Great." I know I'm blushing. "How about you?"

"Best sleep ever."

He kisses me again but pulls away when his phone dings from the kitchen table.

"Will you see who that is?" he asks, flipping the bacon. "I've texted a couple people to see if they can cover for me this week. I hope that's one of them."

"You're going to try to have someone cover all your shifts?" I hand him his phone but not before checking the text

"Yeah, it's the easier solution than finding him a sitter every night."

"I can watch him when I'm not at the gym. The only night I work is Thursday. I work mornings the rest of the week. It's your sister," I say and set the phone on the counter next to him.

"I really appreciate that you want to—"

"Conner, let me help you. I knew you had a son when I met you, remember? I want to help."

He eyes me, taking in my outfit. His throat bobs as he swallows, giving me a quick kiss before turning around to face the stove.

"You're too good to me, Alex, you know that?"

"Yeah, but I like to think I'm just returning the gesture."

This causes him to chuckle.

"Oh, I need to check my mail. I'll be right back. Want me to get yours?" he asks.

"No," I answer a lot faster than necessary. If he checks my mail, then he'll see my last name. Something he should have asked me for by now. It concerns me a little, but it's also a relief that I haven't had to share anything I'm not ready for. Although after last night …

"You sure?"

"Positive."

Tomorrow. I'll tell him tomorrow. What harm can one more day do, right?

CHAPTER TEN

Conner

I have two goals once inventory check is finished: the first is going next door to see if I can find anything with Alex's name on it. We're way too far in now; I can't ask her these questions without looking like it's a second thought or something, and that can never turn out well. The second thing I am going to do is tell Alex about Heather's idea of a family and how it won't work and has nothing to do with her, but that is why Jake's mom has been hard to deal with lately. Maybe Alex will have advice for me. All I know is that if someone tells her before I do, it won't be good.

I should have told her about Heather by now, and vice versa. I can't even think straight long enough to do the right thing anymore. What's gotten into me?

"Is Abby coming in? I swear that girl and inventory are not a good combination. We should just stop scheduling her." Logan steps around the bar, crossing something off the checklist in front of him.

Here he is concerned about inventory, when little does he know his sister is most likely my neighbor and the girl I'm dating.

"Hey, so, have you tried to contact your sister again? I mean, now that Sara is pregnant, doesn't it make you wish you had her around?"

He looks over his clipboard at me and sighs.

"I've thought about it, but honestly, she would have responded by now if she wanted anything to do with me."

"But if she were to, say, walk through that door right now, how would you feel?"

His eyes roam to the door. He stares at it, probably thrown by my sudden interest in his sister.

He shrugs.

"I'd be happy, I guess."

"You guess?" I'm not appreciating the uncertainty in his voice. If Alex really is his sister, no wonder she hasn't told him or anyone else. But it still stings a little that she won't tell me.

"No, yeah, I'd be thrilled." He sounds surer this time and shakes his head as if to dismiss the thought. "Why does it matter? It's not going to happen."

"Yeah, you're right." I, too, erase the idea from my head. No doubt he would keep that off-limits rule for sisters into play, and I don't feel like taking my chances. Maybe subconsciously that's why I haven't asked her. If she says yes, I'd be breaking the pact Logan and I made as kids.

"So," I change the subject. "I invited Alex to your house this weekend. I hope nothing comes up this time."

"Me too. Sara and I both want to meet this girl. I heard—after a few others gossiped, of course, so correct me if I'm wrong—but I heard the two of you and Jake were looking quite the family the other day in the park. Could it be you've found someone Heather approves of?"

I cringe. Here I am, the guy who hates secrets, and I'm keeping two myself. Three, if you count the fact Alex could be Logan's sister and I should tell him about her. When did I become so selfish?

"Heather doesn't know," I say, guiding the subject away from Alex.

Logan nods slowly. A good minute passes before he says anything.

"Look, I don't know this girl, but I know you and I've seen a difference in you since she moved in."

"How?"

"You're relaxed. You're definitely not as crabby as you were before when you came to work, and you seem happy."

He's right. I just never realized how much the people around me observed my emotions.

"If she means that much to you, you have to tell Heather. End of story."

He disappears into the back, and I spend the next hour counting bottles and tracking numbers at the front of the bar.

I need to trust Alex. She would have told me by now if she were Logan's sister. She's had plenty of chances. We're honest with each other. That's exactly why I will tell her about Heather tonight first thing when I get off. If I confide in her, it's possible that could be the push she needs to open up. She'll trust me like I trust her.

I know she will.

* * *

I'm stepping out of my truck outside the apartment at the same time Alex pulls in. She gets out, slams her door, and then grabs a few grocery bags from the back seat, slamming that door also.

"Is everything okay?" I ask, stealing the bags from her to carry them inside.

"No." She throws her hands in the air. "Did you know Abby has a history of ruining relationships?"

She's pissed.

"Yes, I did know that."

"Not only with your sister, but with your best friend, too. Crazy. I just can't believe it. I wanted to see the best in her, but I just can't now. How could anyone do that? You make a commitment; you should keep it. As both a friend and a significant other."

"I completely agree."

"How could she even want to come between a happy couple? I can't wrap my head around it."

"I'm not defending her, but it's not only her fault. There is always a second party to making the wrong choice." I wait behind her as she unlocks her door. "Both people have to want to make a relationship work for it to work."

"So, say a guy doesn't like his girl anymore. It's okay for him to cheat?"

"No, that's not what I'm saying."

"It's just wrong to come between people like that. I mean, say Heather wanted to be with you. It would be wrong of me to be doing whatever this is that we're doing with you."

Oh, this isn't good.

"How do you figure that?"

"Because I'd be that girl who came between a family. We've had this conversation before."

"Yeah, but refresh my memory." I set the bags on her counter and watch as she puts food away and talks at the same time.

"It just is. It's like first come, first serve. She was here first, so the right thing would be for me to back away if the occasion presented itself."

"I don't agree with you."

"You don't have to. That's just how I feel."

"For this particular circumstance, I do think we should agree," I say. If I can't get her to see why her logic makes no sense, I won't be sharing anything with her today.

"What if I never came along? How do you know that you and Heather would never get together?"

"Because I don't have feelings for her. That's how I know. She's Jake's mom, that's all."

I slide against the counter, pausing in front of where she's leaning, and rest my hands on her hips.

"You, however, I like very much."

"You're just saying that to change the subject." She pecks a kiss against my lips. "But you're right, what I'm saying doesn't even make sense. I'm just worked up is all, and my mind is all over the place. The last thing I want to think about is you and Jake's mom."

That settles it.

"That, I do agree with. Right now, I'd rather do what I spent most of my day thinking about." Holding onto her hips, I lift her onto the counter, separating her legs to rest myself between them as I kiss her, hard.

I'll make sure we come back to this conversation at a later date.

Alexis

Conner's hands run up the tops of my thighs, pushing the fabric of my dress back. When they reach my backside he grips my butt, pulling me forward, and crashes my center against his.

"I've been thinking about this all damn day," he groans into my ear.

"I almost showed up on your lunch hour. I've been thinking about this moment since I woke up," I confess. My words send him into overdrive as his hands make quick work with his zipper.

My hands tug at his hair as my tongue slides into his mouth, meeting his own with each kiss. Our lips move as though not kissing would rip us up. As if pulling away would ruin us for the rest of our lives.

I gasp loudly as a finger slides between my legs. The motion spreads my legs even farther. His lips feather kisses along my neck, jawline, and against my ear. Another moan escapes my lips.

"Fuck, I'm sorry, I wanted to drag this out, but I don't think I can."

My ass lifts and my panties are swooped down and off my legs before he's even finished his sentence. He picks me up, walking us to the sofa, where he sits with me on top of him. As he slowly rests back against the couch, I lower myself on to him.

A hiss comes from deep in his throat once I'm as far as I can go.

"I'll never get used to that," he whispers into my ear.

I start to rock myself against him. His hands are at my hips, helping to control the movement. Each time I start to go fast, he slows me down by gripping my body and groaning as his head leans back.

He stops me, completely lifting me off him and turning me to place my hands on the back of the couch as he stands behind me.

He thrusts hard and I cry out, enjoying every pleasurable moment he gives me. His hands sneak around to cup my breasts as he kisses my neck. His hips move faster and harder as his body crashes against mine from behind. My entire body shudders, and I feel as though I'm going to black out the moment my orgasm hits me. His quickened pace and groan before he slows lets me know he felt it, too.

"What are you doing to me?" He laughs, pulling up his jeans and pulling down my dress before he heads for the bathroom. He comes out and laces our fingers as he sits next to me. "I've never felt so out of control the way I feel when I'm with you," he says.

"As lame as this sounds, I think it's us more than it is one person."

A deep chuckle comes from his throat. He turns to look at me, but his eyes catch sight of something else. The moment I see him reach for my mail on the table, I straddle his lap.

"I'm not sure we're finished," I say, distracting him and shaming myself for leaving something so stupid out in the open.

When he looks me in the eye, I see the question there. The

one asking me what I'm hiding, but I can't answer him. Instead, I kiss him and I don't stop kissing him until his sister calls to tell him she's here with Jake.

When he leaves, I can think only one thing: every day that I don't tell him, I'm making things worse, and there is good chance this won't end well.

CHAPTER ELEVEN

Alexis

From the moment Conner reminded me about this get together at his friend's house, I've felt this weird vibe. Like he was nervous I was going to say no. His hands have been twisting around the steering wheel for the entire drive, and he hasn't spoken but a few words here and there. Normally I'd let his odd actions pass and not think another thing of it, but his nervousness is making me worry. There's only one way to address this: ask him the obvious question and hope that his answer isn't the one I believe it is. I never asked him whose house we were going to—because who has a barbeque twice a month?—but right now, I wish I would have done that before we got in the truck.

"Conner, is everything okay?" Although this isn't my question, easing into the one I want to ask is probably the best idea.

"Yeah," he answers quickly, not pulling his eyes away from the road to look at me. Safety is good, but he's always been the kind of person to make eye contact when he talks. Avoiding it isn't a good sign. When he doesn't add to his answer, I get the feeling he knows, and I get right to the point.

"Whose house are we going to?"

"A friend's."

"What kind of friend?"

"It's Logan's house," he blurts out.

Crap. I knew it. I can't meet him now. I'm not ready to do this. What is Conner thinking, bringing me here? Oh that's right, he has no idea because I've kept it a secret. Unless he does know, and then this is awful.

"Like, the same couple who own the bar you work at?" It's a stupid question, I know, but I'm secretly hoping he knows another Logan.

"Yes, and I know how you feel about the whole thing, but Logan is my best friend and I really want you two to meet."

"I'm not feeling well. I think you should take me home."

"What?" At the same moment he pulls his truck into the driveway of a medium-sized dark blue house with brown trim. From the outside it looks as though it might be a bi-level. I can tell it definitely has an upstairs from the giant window in the arch.

There are a group of people huddled around the middle of three garage doors and a group of women near the front door. I immediately recognize Beth and Kelsey, but the other woman, the one with blonde hair curled and flowing like waterfall to the middle of her back, I don't know. But I have a pretty good idea who she is. She's another person I'm not ready to meet.

"We have to leave," I say, quickly. My body temperature

rises and I feel the lunch I had earlier fighting its way to come up. "Now, please. Get me out of here now!"

Somewhere in the three sentences I've managed to say since we arrived, I've started to cry and Beth has noticed us. She's now looking at me with a puzzled expression as Conner backs out of the driveway.

"Alex, I need you to explain what happened just now." His voice is calm and sweet, but I still don't answer. There is only one way for me to explain this without sounding like I've totally lost my mind. I'm going to have to tell him the truth.

"Just at least nod to tell me it's not a life-or-death situation."

Isn't it, though? What happens when Logan decides he doesn't want me to be a part of his life? Or what happens if it turns out I'm not really his sister and the letter was a fake?

Still, I nod.

We drive in silence, the same way as before until we reach the apartment. I head for my door and Conner for his. If I don't do this now, I'll never find the courage to do it again, and if I don't tell him something, anything, about what just happened, whatever this is between us could be ruined.

"Conner, if you want to come over for a minute, I'd like to explain some things to you." I say the words slowly, as if I need to say them to myself to reassure in my own mind that this needs to happen. Maybe by telling Conner, I'll be one step closer to telling Logan.

His step falters as his gaze meets mine. Worry and frustration take over his beautiful face. Finally, he nods and follows me inside. I point to the sofa and then take a seat across from him.

"Why have you never asked what my last name is?" I ask.

"It's easy to see that you are still guarding yourself from me. I don't know what this is, but I never asked you too many personal questions because I didn't want to ruin whatever we have."

"And I adore you for that, Conner, but I didn't just come here for a fresh start on a new life." I slide a magazine on the table toward him, waiting until he reads it over. The moment he sees my name, Alexis Parker, I expect him to be furious, but instead, he's the total opposite.

"So it's true? You really are Logan's sister."

I can see in the way he slouches into one of my kitchen table chairs that he's hurt. I should have told him sooner.

"I came here to find my brother, and he just so happens to be your best friend. I didn't plan that, but I'm glad you're friends with him."

The way his lips twitch, I can see he's fighting the urge to smile. Sooner than I'd like, the urge is gone and the frustration is back.

"Why didn't you tell me?"

"I didn't want anyone to know."

"Why not?"

"I didn't want anyone to treat me differently once they knew."

"Not even me?"

"Especially you. Logan's your best friend, and I knew if I told you, you'd make me tell him."

"You're not going to tell him?"

"No."

His hand curls into a fist on the table as he lets out a breath. Now his voice is low and firm.

"Logan looked for you for over a year. Not finding you

tore him up. It caused problems with him and Sara, and he sacrificed a lot for you. And here you are, in the same town, and you don't even have the respect for him to tell him who you are."

"Conner, it's not that easy. I'm not ready to admit to him that I'm here."

"Why not?"

"I'm just not ready."

"You're not ready to tell your brother that the family he searched for, the family he thinks wants nothing to do with him, came to Wind Valley to find him?"

"Yes, and I'd really appreciate if you kept this between us." The last word comes out almost in a whisper. I know how he feels about secrets, or holding the truth from someone. Asking him to do this is asking him to go against everything he is.

The gaze that usually seeps right into my soul and warms my heart turns cold and angry. I have to look away before I start crying again.

"You can't be serious."

"I know how it sounds, but—"

"Nothing good will come from keeping this to yourself, Alexis Parker." The bitter way he says my full name stings. "I don't want to be a part of it. Either you tell Logan or I will."

He doesn't wait for me to respond before he exits my apartment. I don't even know what I would have said if he had waited. He's right; I need to tell Logan. I just hope Conner gives me the time I need to do it on my own.

Conner

It's been a week since Alex told me she's Logan sister. *Alexis.* She'll always be just Alex to me. I shouldn't have doubted it for so long. I should have just manned up and asked her about it. Been there for her instead letting it dwell in my mind or walking out on her when she did finally admit the truth.

Every day I wait for Logan's call to either tell me about it or ask me how long I knew. Each day that phone call doesn't come, it becomes harder for me to not say anything.

I know I should let her do it, but she wasn't here. She doesn't know what Logan went through. Although he never came out and told me he decided to give up, all the signs were there, and I'll never forget the way he acted.

My phone rings and the hope that it's Logan strikes again.

It's not. It's Alex.

I press the ignore button, the same way I've done since she told me. We weren't even officially dating, but the fact that she couldn't trust me, that even after everything I told her she still kept it a secret, pains me. Was she ever really listening to me, or was she just using me to get closer to Logan?

I'm such a coward for acting this way when I have things of my own I'm keeping from her.

I shake the thought the moment I have it. Alex and Logan haven't even met, that I know of, so it's impossible she could have been using me. Still, another woman I brought into my life didn't trust me enough to let me into her own.

"Knock, knock." Heather's voice comes from my doorway. Jake runs in, his hair spiked and his Ninja Turtle backpack half the size of him bounces off his legs as he jumps on the couch next to me.

"Dad! Mom said I was staying for a whole week! How cool is that!" Every word that comes out his mouth is filled with excitement. There is no possible way I can be anything but happy when he's around. My feeling toward his mother however, is not so happy. She picked him up for two days from my parents' house no less, probably avoiding me. And now, something new apparently came up, and he's back. His mother's lack of commitment to him these last two weeks is not okay.

"Yeah, bud, it's a boys' weekend for sure," I say, but he's already focused on pulling some toys out of his backpack.

"I'll be back on Thursday," Heather says, still standing in the doorway. I get off the couch to join her.

"I need to talk to you about something," I say as she turns to leave.

"Can it wait? I really have to go."

"No, it can't wait." I follow her out into the hallway, leaving the door cracked so Jake can't hear us but just in case he needs me.

"You'll have to call me," she says.

"Heather, no, we need to talk."

"Call me." She exits through the building door. I follow her.

"Heather!" She doesn't stop and I'm not going to chase her down.

"Dad?"

"Yeah?" I turn. Jake is standing in the hallway, leaning against the wall, bouncing from his butt to his back as he talks. "You said this was a boys' weekend."

"Sure is," I say with a smile.

"What about Alex? She isn't a boy."

I swallow then, my heart tugging at the way his bummed out voice recognizes that we won't be hanging out with Alex.

"No, bud, we won't. Maybe next time," I tell him, praying inside that Alex tells Logan soon. I want to hang out with her, too.

Jake watches me for a moment, his little brown eyes looking at me like he knows I'm keeping something from him. He's quickly distracted, and the moment he sits back on the couch, that's when it hits me.

My chest aches at the mess things are in right now and my fist is curled and digging into the couch cushions. Five minutes. That's all I needed. I wanted to be respectful and talk to Heather in person, but if she won't let that happen, then over the phone it is. The fact I haven't told her and the fact I can't confront anyone is making things worse.

That's going to change.

CHAPTER TWELVE

Conner

I texted Heather early this morning, asking her to call me when she had a free moment today, seeing as how she wouldn't answer my calls again last night. At 3:00 p.m. on the dot, my phone vibrates in my hand. I press the green button, accepting the call and praying for the best.

"Hello?" I sound like an idiot because I know who it is.

"Conner, you wanted me to call you?" There's a hopeful tone to her voice that stabs me.

"Yes, I just wanted to talk to you about us and the suggestion you made a few weeks ago."

"Okay, I'm free now. Where do you want to start?"

I take a nice, deep breath and release it as calmly as I possibly can. *Please let this go well.*

"A while ago, the apartment across from me was rented out and the woman who moved in—" I stop right there. This is not the best way to start this. I have to tell her, yeah, but just in case she uses Jake against me, I still need to be nice about it.

"Alright, so, I don't think our becoming a couple is the best idea for us or for Jake." Yeah, okay, that sounds better.

For a second, she doesn't respond.

"You don't?" Her voice is soft and then I hear her sniffle.

"I love Jake with all my heart. Don't ever doubt that. But, Heather, I don't have those same feelings for you, and you deserve someone who is going to love you that way. We both do."

"But we can get there. We have a son together. Doesn't it mean something to give this a try?"

"It does, yes, as long as both parties want it."

"And you don't want me. You don't want a family with me and Jake. He deserves it. You won't even do it for him?"

"Even if I did this for him, it wouldn't be fair to him. He needs parents who are happy and who get along. That's where we are now and I don't want to ruin it by forcing something that isn't there."

"But it's there with this new person, who moved in across from you. Was that where you were going with that? That you fell in love with someone else?"

Am I in love?

I run my hand over my face. Going into detail about Alex wasn't part of my plan, but I guess I messed that up the moment I opened my mouth.

"It's Logan's sister." I say each word slowly. It's the first time I've said it out loud.

"I wasn't aware he had a sister."

"Yeah, she's younger than him." I scratch the back of my neck as I push off the couch and lean against the counter.

Silence takes over the phone call.

"Is she attractive?"

The question catches me off guard, causing me to hesitate on my answer, which apparently isn't the right answer right now.

"An attractive woman is going to distract you from your son, Conner."

"Nothing will distract me from my son."

"You don't know that, I know it."

"Heather, I swear to you, Jake is and will always be my first priority."

"Conner—"

"Trust me." My voice raises and immediately I regret it. This is not how I wanted this conversation to go. "Please," I say, my voice much more calm and pleading.

"Fine, but I don't like it. I don't like knowing my son is around another woman when he isn't with me."

"Alex is great with him; you have nothing to worry about."

"Can I meet her?" This questions throw me completely off. "Please, for peace of mind. When I bring Jake over next weekend."

"Okay," I answer. Alex will understand. "As long as she isn't working at the gym, she should be here."

We hang up and I sigh with relief. Our conversation didn't go anything close to what I had imagined it would, and I also covered a second dreaded topic. Now, I just need to patch things up with Alex so she can meet Heather. I should probably not start by mentioning this conversation.

. . .

Alexis

Conner doesn't answer my phone call, again. I consider texting him but there is no emotion in a text and I want him to know and hear that I'm serious. I'm going to tell Logan soon, and I'd really like it if Conner would help me out with what I'm going to say, because everything he said was right. I need to tell Logan and I have to stop pretending like I'm the only person whose life this is going to affect. Conner never actually said those words, but they were definitely implied about the choices I've made up to this point.

As usual, I clock in when I get to work and head to the back to take the pool temperatures. I put out fresh towels and pick up random hand weights, jump ropes, and any other workout tools left unattended before heading back to the front. If tonight could stay busy until I got off, that would be fantastic. I plan to go to Conner when I get off and I don't need to spend my entire night stressing over how he might react.

"Boyfriend troubles?" Pete asks when I pass the CrossFit area and the indoor track where a younger couple is running laps.

"I'm sorry?" I ask. Pete hasn't ever shown the interest Abby said he had for me the day I met him, so I'm not upset he's asking about Conner. It does, however, bother me that he assumes something is wrong.

"You just look lost in thought, and I since I have a sister, I've seen the look before," he says.

"Oh, well, no, everything is great."

"I've also heard that fake 'I'm not going to tell you about it' answer before, too."

Shoot.

"Look, you don't have to tell me what happened if you don't want to, but I am a good listener if you change your mind."

I'm about to apologize when a woman turns the corner near the yoga studio. She has short, dark hair and porcelain skin that reminds me of a girl named Heather I grew up with in my last foster home. She smiles, gaining my full attention. Pete walks around us without another word.

"Alexis?" the woman asks when I'm close enough to touch her. I pause to get a better look—she *is* the same girl from my foster home. Her face lights up, probably a mimicked reaction to my own, and we hug.

"Oh my gosh! This is crazy. What are you doing here?" she asks excitedly. Her smile is bright and familiar. It's been way too long since I've seen someone from my past life, and it feels both nice and weird. Heather was one of the kindest people to me growing up. Foster kids can be hard to live with because we all have such different backgrounds and stories to tell, but Heather was accepting of everyone.

"I live here now," I say.

"Are you serious? That's unbelievable. We have to get lunch or coffee or something to catch up."

"Yeah, that would be really nice."

"This is just too crazy." She keeps smiling. "How did you end up here?"

I laugh. "I should be asking you the same question, but I actually just moved here a month or so ago. My real brother lives here and I came here to reconnect with him."

Her smile slowly fades. "Interesting."

"Yeah." What started as an exciting conversation immediately gets awkward.

"Well, I better get to class," she says. "Good luck with your brother. I'll stop by the front on my way out to plan coffee."

"Okay," I say to her backside because she's already halfway down the hall.

Of all the kids I met growing up, I shared more secrets with Heather than anyone else about the life I wished for. I can't wait to talk to her and see what life has brought her since we parted ways.

* * *

When I get home, I park my car and notice the living room light in Conner's apartment is on. The television is on and I can see his silhouette lying on the couch.

I can do this. Whatever Conner and I have goes way past a silly fight. He'll understand. I need to start trusting this gut feeling I have.

I knock on his door with a shaky hand. He mutes the TV. Then his door is open and he's standing before me looking hot as hell in just a pair of sweats. I take a deep breath and force my eyes to remain glued to his instead of them allowing them to roam the smooth sight of his naked and hard chest.

"Hey," I say the way I say it every time I see him. I even give him a half smile, hoping he doesn't shut me out. "Can we talk?"

He nods, stepping to the side and gesturing for me to come in. He closes the door and then strides past me, taking his spot back on the couch. I get it. He's waiting for me to start. Which since technically I'm the only one who has any apologizing to do, it only makes sense.

I sit next to him, resting my purse on my lap and looking down at it.

"I'm going to tell Logan."

This grabs his attention.

"I'm going to tell him this week. I don't know when or how, but I am going to do it. It's what I came here for, and you were right, he deserves to know. I'm just …" I take a deep breath as more tears prick at my eyes and I pull Logan's letter from my purse. "I'm scared that the brother who wrote me this letter isn't the same brother anymore. What if the fact he's married and about to start a family has focused him on the future, and he doesn't want his past to come back?"

Conner inches over until his arms are wrapped around me. My body leans into his and I cry into his chest.

"He isn't going to reject you." He kisses the top of my head. "It's not possible. You are his sister and you're an amazing person. He's watched the way you've changed my life. He's going to love you."

I dry my eyes enough to look up at him.

"How could I have changed your life? We've only know each other for a few weeks."

"Probably for the same reason you came to me tonight. Because you're the person I want to know my secrets. You're the person who, yes, in just weeks, has managed to take over more of my heart than anyone I know, excluding Jake, of course."

A small laugh bubbles up from my throat. I then let out a sigh of relief. Tilting my chin until I'm looking at him, Conner kisses me. It's a soft and gentle kiss that gives me all the reassurance I need. Conner is going to be there for me and I don't need to worry anymore.

"I have an idea," he says breaking the kiss and wiping away my last few tears with his thumb. "Tell me something you would tell Logan."

"I don't know. Won't that be awkward?"

"Is that what you're worried about? Things being awkward between you and Logan?"

"I'm not worried about it; I expect it."

"Alright, good point, but I'll probably have a different reaction than what you're expecting Logan to have."

"Sooo, you want to have like a practice talk? With you playing my brother?" I cock my eyebrow.

"Um, no. Definitely not as your brother. Just as Conner, but yeah, sure, shoot. Practice on me."

"Okay," I reply, hesitating over what my first question should be. When I take too long to answer, Conner beats me to it.

"How many foster homes did you stay in?"

"Four. It took a while before someone decided I was good enough to keep," I say, my head down.

"Why didn't you move out of the last one when you were eighteen?" he asks another question before I can ask one in return. I scoot back on his couch, taking my jacket off and crossing my legs Indian style. The fact he knows this information confirms my curiosity on whether or not Logan talked to anyone about me. Also, it warms my heart to know Logan put an effort into searching for me.

"I was their last foster child. They wanted to retire, but I think a part of them was going to miss the whole child-caring thing. So they told me I could stay if I wanted to."

"They were good people?" he asks. These questions seem

too easy for him. I get the sense that maybe these are topics he's been wanting to ask since I told him.

"Better than some of the foster homes. We didn't have nice things, but we did have everything we needed. When they gave me the option to stay, I took it because it was the smart thing to do. I planned to move some day, but money wasn't something that came easy. I stayed with them and got a job, eventually moved out. Now, here I am."

"That's good to hear. You should tell Logan about all that. He'd love to hear they treated you well."

He's right. Logan probably does wonder all the same things I do.

"Um," I begin, tucking hair behind my ear. "Were Logan's foster parents good to him?"

My eyes slowly flutter back in Conner's direction and when they meet his, he stands.

"That's something you should talk to Logan about, and the questions you have for him, you should write down. That way, if you forget because you're too nervous, you have something to focus on."

"That's a pretty good idea you have there, Mr. Brian," I say, rising to stand in front of him.

"I thought so myself, Ms. Parker."

The moment his lips touch mine once again, I let my entire body relax into his embrace. Meeting Conner is one of the best things that could have happened to me. I'm not a huge believer in fate, but I may need to start. I don't think I was meant to come here just for my brother. I think I was meant to meet Conner, too. Someone is looking out for me and as long as I have Conner on my side, I'll be okay.

<h1 style="text-align:center">CHAPTER THIRTEEN</h1>

Conner

Alex's leg bounces as she sits next to me on the couch.

"You need to stop worrying. I promise, it's going to be okay."

I rub my hand across her back in an attempt to calm her down. She's been here for less than ten minutes and we've yet to leave the apartment.

After our conversation a couple days ago, I mentioned that if she's this worried over Logan's reaction, maybe meeting him in a place where he is most comfortable is a good idea. It was either his house or the BA, and Alex chose the BA because of its location to her own apartment.

I called him last night to ask if he and Sara wanted to get together for a lunch date so I could finally introduce them to Alex. They both agreed that it's about time because, according to them, if I'm not talking about Jake, I'm talking about her.

"I think we should re-schedule," she says, slouching back and resting her face in her hands. "I can't do it. Just thinking about it makes me want to throw up. I mean, what if he starts yelling or accusing me of lying, or what if he does believe me and tells me he doesn't want me to be a part of his life anymore because this is too much for him?" She begins to pace. "How am I going to react to that? I won't be able to stay here. I'll have to move and it will all have been for nothing and I'll be back where I was before with nothing and I don't know if I can handle the rejection."

"Okay, just take a deep breath." I stand, stopping her in the center of my living room and rubbing my hands down her arms. "I've known Logan for as long as I can remember. He's my best friend and one of the most understanding people I know. He won't reject you."

"But—"

"I told you." I cut her words off with a kiss on her forehead. "I was there when he tried to find you. He may have stopped trying, but that was only because he never heard from you and thought that's what you wanted. So he left you alone."

She's nodding and keeps nodding as she looks around. "Okay, yeah, let's go before I change my mind."

"Good. I'll drive so you can't bolt if you get scared." This earns me an eye roll. She nudges me and then heads out the door.

She's worried Logan won't accept her. I get it. I also know she's got nothing to worry about. Me, on the other hand, I'm pretty sure I need to worry. He'll be accepting of her all right, but of us, I'm not so sure.

Time to find out.

* * *

I park in my usual spot on the side of the building. The moment the engine is turned off and my hand is on the door handle, Alex rests her hand on my arm to stop me.

"Thank you for coming with me." Her eyes start to glaze over and it's right now, in this moment, I realize she trusts me. It may have taken her a while, but she told me everything. And yet I can't find the words to tell her about Jake's mom. I know it doesn't matter, but she deserves to know. There is never the right time for a topic like that and this is definitely not the right moment, but I have to man up sooner rather than later.

I open my mouth, but I don't get any words out before her lips are on mine. She leans her entire body into the kiss, slipping her tongue into my mouth. The feeling goes right to my groin. I lean back, reaching my hand around her head and holding her lips to mine as I deepen the kiss. Anytime we kiss, it's easy to get lost, to forget where I am or what is the right thing to do. I should stop this, but I don't want to.

The fist pounding against my window, however, does.

"Hey! Are we eating lunch or what?" Logan glares at us through the window.

I jerk away from Alex and she does the same. She looks straight out the passenger's window away from Logan. I nod and give him a finger, letting him know we'll be just a minute.

He nods, turning to open Sara's door and they disappear inside the building.

"Okay, now I definitely can't tell him."

"Why not?"

"Umm, hello, Conner, you were here. The first time I see my brother after all these years and it's because he caught me making out with his best friend!"

"Sounds like pretty typical brother-sister behavior. You guys will be fine."

"Conner." She shoves me against the door. Well, attempts to as she laughs. "This isn't funny."

"Alex, come on, think about it. This is the moment you came to Wind Valley for. You can't back out now. You both deserve this. And if, that's a big if, it doesn't go the way you planned, the stress of never knowing will still be gone."

"You're right."

"But don't worry. It's going to be fine."

She finally gets out of the truck, with me right behind her. I lace our fingers as we go inside. A way to remind her that I am here for her. Logan waves from a table near the jukebox. Alex looks up at me one more time before we head in their direction.

I pull out her chair when we get to the table and clear my throat.

"Sara, help me pick out a song."

"What?" she and Logan say in unison.

"A song."

"Go pick one out yourself." Logan squints his eyes at me.

"I want Sara's opinion on changing some of the choices."

"Are you being serious?" she asks.

This is not working out as well as I hoped it would.

"Sara, please?" I use my most polite yet just-do-it voice. This earns me an eye roll from Logan and I almost laugh. These two are so much alike. He's going to love this.

I step away from the table, guiding Sara toward the jukebox with quick steps.

"Geez, Conner, what is going on?"

"Alex is Alexis."

"Your point? Everyone has nicknames."

"Alexis Parker."

Her eyes go wide and she looks back to the table.

"She's been scared to—"

"Shhhh! I want to hear them."

And just like that I'm shushed as I wait for Alex to reveal her secret. I hope it goes well. I hope it goes really well that he's so happy to finally have his sister, that he doesn't mind me dating her. And I really hope it goes well because I've never been so nervous for someone else in my life.

Alexis

Conner isn't the smoothest guy. I've kept my head down since his first awkward invitation for Sara to join him came out of his mouth. With them away from the table, I glance up.

Logan smiles as he extends his hand. The moment I lift my chin and look him straight on, his entire body freezes. His eyes survey me from the other side of the table. I wait for confusion to set in, because that's what I prepared myself for. I definitely didn't expect him to recognize me so quickly. His throat bobs as he swallows, never removing his eyes from mine.

"Hi, Logan. I'm Alexis Parker," I say, placing my hand in his. He continues to look at me with wide eyes. It both freaks me out and makes me want to break into tears. My heart is beating so hard it hurts my ears.

"I'm your sister."

Silence and a slight jaw drop is all I get. I wait. I look around for Conner and find him and Sara both watching us like it's a live movie. I start to scoot my chair back, because it's obvious I was right and I didn't make the best judgment call. Conner steps up to the table. He stands next to my chair and motions for me to stop. He tilts his head toward Logan, who is still staring at me.

"Do you want me to go?" I ask.

Logan finally snaps out of his state of shock and shakes his head.

"No, no I don't. I just … this um … this wasn't what I was expecting today."

"Trust me, it's probably just as hard for me to say it to you as it is for you to hear it."

"Why do you say that?"

"Because I got your letter over a year ago and I'm just now showing up. Well, I've been here for a while, but yeah."

He's smiling. but his wide eyes tell me he's still in shock. "You got my letters?" he asks.

"Letters?" He sent me more than one? "No, I only got one." I pull it from my purse, my heart slowing down to its normal pace, but my hands continue to shake. I cried every time I read this letter and each time I tried to dream up how this moment would go. None of them will ever compare to the real thing.

He leans back in his chair and his grin grows. "I can't believe you kept it."

"Someone wanted me to be a part of their family." I shrug. "I couldn't *not* take the chance." My hands shake as I focus on the fact it's possible I've revealed too much for the first five minutes of our meeting. I watch as he takes the letter, unfolds it, and laughs.

"My handwriting looks so awful. I remember shaking the entire time I wrote this. I wasn't sure how many chances I would get. With every word I wrote I told myself I had to get it right."

His voice catches in a few spots and he, too, takes a deep breath. I knew this moment was going to be tough for me and that it would be a shock for him too.

"There is so much I want to ask you, I just don't know if I can do it today," he shares with me and it's the glazed expression in his eyes that makes me realize how much I focused on him having a negative reaction, never considering what it would look like if he were happy to see me.

I'm about to reach out and grab his hand to tell there isn't a reason to hurry because we are brother and sister and we're in this together, but his chair shoots out and he rushes around the table, throwing his arms around me.

I try to do my best to hug him back, but he's squeezing me tighter than ever I expected a guy to hug someone.

"Are we interrupting?" Conner asks. Sara is standing next to him with seriously the happiest smile I've ever seen, and I'm instantly smiling back.

"Oh, damn it," she says looking away and fanning her hand in front of her eyes. "I'm so sorry, I just … okay, okay, and I'm good now."

"Alexis, this is my wife, Sara. Babe, this is Alexis, my sister."

I don't even have time to reply before she, too, is swinging her arms around me. "Oh, this is so amazing. You look just like him, but you know, female and beautiful."

"Hey, I'm beautiful," Logan says behind her.

"No, you're handsome," she replies.

He kisses Sara on the temple and then she smiles up at

him. He looks happy, and knowing that he's had her in his life makes a small piece of me feel relieved.

"Oh shoot, you're not going to cry, too, are you?" Sara asks, grabbing a napkin off the table and handing it to me. I wasn't even aware any tears had slipped by.

"I'm crying because I'm pregnant and apparently that's my only symptom and it's in high gear all day, every day," Sara admits, taking the seat next to me. She leans over, resting her head on my shoulder, apparently already comfortable with me. I've heard so much about her, so many good things, that I enjoy the gesture.

Logan returns to his seat and Conner takes the one across from me. He reaches over to squeeze my hands in his. I don't miss the slight glare Logan gives him.

"Can we still eat?" Sara asks. We all laugh, and just like that, I'm having lunch with my brother and it feels like a huge brick had been taken off my back.

I know it's only day one of an entire relationship we have to build, but between Logan and Conner, I've never felt so at home. Nothing could ruin this.

CHAPTER FOURTEEN

Conner

The best mornings are those when you don't have to wake up to an alarm or anything else before your body actually wants to rise and greet the day. Don't get me wrong, I love my son, but waking up on lazy mornings to the sun peeking through the windows and a very sexy, leggy, and naked woman wrapped up in your sheets is real nice, too.

Alex and I are curled up, her back to my front. At some point during the night we must have shifted away from each other. I reach over her and tug her body back into mine. She lets out a sigh so I know she's awake, then she lets out moan to let me know how awake she is.

"I thought we were sleeping in today," she says with a sleepy voice. She rolls over to face me and touches her lips to my nose.

"It's almost ten. Technically, you already did sleep in." I kiss her softly, rolling halfway on top of her.

"Before you distract me, I want to thank you for helping me talk to Logan."

"Anything for you." I kiss her again.

"I mean it, if I hadn't told you, or, technically, if you hadn't figured it out, I'd still be alone inside my apartment stressing on what I'm going to about Logan. Instead, now I have all day to think about what I want to do next, with you."

"And what have you come up with so far?"

"Well, it involves you and water and being naked."

Without a second thought I roll out of bed, pulling the sheet and Alex with me, and I lift her over my shoulder and head for the bathroom. The landlord fixed her shower yesterday. We're pretending he didn't.

"Conner, I'm not done talking yet," she laughs, wigging in my hold as I step into the bathroom.

"We can talk later." I silence her with my lips. Logan is the last person I want to be thinking about in my shower. Especially since my focus should be on how I'm going to convince him that the "never date a sister" rule can't apply to me and Alex.

Logan gets right into it when he spots me behind the bar. "The sister rule still applies, you know."

"You're positive this girl is your sister?" I ask, joking with him. Maybe approaching it with a lighter tone will make the conversation easier on both of us. There is no way the rule can still be held against me the same way. Not after I've already been with Alex, and he clearly caught us making out last weekend when Alex told him the truth. This is one promise I'm going to have to break.

"Dude, did you see her? She looks like just like me only the female version." He clearly didn't pick up on my joke. "Same blonde hair, our skin tone is freaking spot on, and we have the same eyes."

The fuck they do. Her eyes hypnotize me. They capture me. They are something I'll never forget. Logan's eyes are ... I glance at him.

Damn, that's weird. Yeah, those are just Logan's eyes.

"The rule can't apply to us," I say. "I'm sorry."

"How can it not apply?"

"We made that pact when we were kids, and at the time ..."

"I didn't have a sister. Yeah, I get it, but she's here now. The rule should still apply."

"Why?"

"Because it should."

He focuses on the wall across from us, in good ole Logan fashion. When he knocks his knuckles against the bar top, it's a dead giveaway that something else is bothering him.

"What is it?" I ask.

"Nothing," he snaps.

"Look me in the eye and tell me the fact that I'm breaking this rule is the only thing that's bothering you."

He opens his mouth to argue but pauses before asking me, "Did you know she was my sister this whole time?"

I don't think that's his problem, either.

"No, I didn't know she was your sister until a week ago."

He lets this sink in for a moment.

"Do you think she needs help? Like maybe she ran from

something and that's why all of a sudden she showed up and took so long to tell anyone. Oh, and you need to get that landlord out to your building stat to fix her plumbing, or you at least need tell me you have some kind of shower rule right now."

It's all about the rules with this guy, and yeah, it's a rule we shower together.

"Shower rule?" I ask, knowing that isn't what he wants to hear. I could tell him that it's fixed, but this is more fun.

"Dude, there will be no chance of you running into my sister in her towel. I've had that situation with Sara too many times to know how it ends and to also know I don't want that for you. At least, I don't want to think about the two of you and whatever thing you have going on right now."

"Okay ..." I begin. It sounds like I'm going to need to take another approach to this topic. I can't leave here today without convincing him that Alexis and I are right for each other and his support would be nice to have. "Stepping into the big brother role ASAP, huh?"

"I've had a lot of years to think about what it would be like to see her again and I really hope she wants the same type of relationship I do," he says before he starts to ramble again. "Do you think she is too skinny?"

"She isn't skinny; her ass is fucking perfect and if you meant—"

"I said the rule still applies. You can't date my sister or even think about anything that involves my sister as more than just your friend. I saw you kissing her. That has to end."

"Logan, come on, this situation is different."

"No, it's not."

"Yeah, it is."

"What, because you met her first? She's my sister, Conner."

"This is different."

"No, no way are you going to give me that speech."

"I get it." I chuckle. "But—"

"If she's dating you, there will be no time for me to get to know her, Conner. And you already know her better than I do, and that's not fair."

And there it is.

"Logan, she wants to know you more than anyone else in the world, even me. I want to be there for her while you get to know each other, and I want to be there to watch as you make memories. Of course, I want to be a part of some of them. But Logan, I'm so into your sister and want to be with her so badly, I'm willing to destroy our entire friendship to make sure I wake up to her smile and her happiness every morning."

Logan's hands are on his hips and his jaw twitches as he grinds his teeth. He keeps his vision focused on me until I've mastered enough of a straight face to convince him I'm serious.

He blows out a quick breath.

"Fine. I'll give it a shot because she did tell me you arranged for us to meet since she was nervous, and because if she is happy with you, I'm not going to take that away. But hear me now: if you do anything, and I mean anything, to hurt her, I get a free pass to hit you as hard as I can whenever I feel like it for the rest of our lives."

"Deal," I say because there is no chance of that ever happening.

When Logan enters the office, leaving me alone, I start

rehearsing how I'm going to tell Alex about Heather wanting us to be a family but that's not going to work and it isn't because of her. If I weren't so happy with Alex and distracted by her smile and touch, I'd have told her by now.

Shit, I've got to stop making excuses.

I have no words to start and I better find them soon or getting Logan's approval was all for nothing and I'll lose Alex and get a punch in the face every day until who knows when.

Alexis

"I still can't believe you're Logan's sister," Beth comments as she lays on my couch. She's drinking a bottle of ginger ale and swinging it by the cap like a drunken person. "I bet Logan cried the moment he and Sara got back to their house."

"Yeah, I doubt that." I laugh off her statement.

The last few days have been … interesting. Logan and I still make things a little awkward with our lack of communication when we're together. There have been a few times where we have done nothing but sit in the same room together in complete silence. Our past is a hard subject to bring up.

Logan adjusting to the idea of me and Conner probably has a little something to do with it as well. He asks me almost every day if Conner's still treating me right. I laugh and tell him yes each time.

Sara and I are chatting about her pregnancy every chance we get, and she's also successfully managed to make me feel welcome even with the way Logan and I act around each other.

"I'm serious. No one would see it if they were a passerby, but Logan has the softest man heart of any guy I know."

She clearly doesn't know Conner that well.

"Are you ready to go?" I ask, opening the door because either way, I'm going to the barbeque at my brother's house. Something they do about every other weekend.

"Eager to see the fam, huh?" She stands, dragging her feet to the door. "I guess that makes sense. If I'd spent my whole life without family, I'd probably want to see them too."

"Yeah, that's it." But really I'm just as excited to see Conner. It's been a busy week and I've been spending a lot of time at Logan and Sara's house. I didn't realize how much I liked Conner until I didn't get to see him as much as I used to. The fact he's come in to sleep next to me the last two nights doesn't count as actually hanging out.

The drive goes fast and before I know it, Beth pulls her car up in front of their house, and my heartbeat speeds up at the sight of all the cars.

"Is it normal for this many people to be here?" I ask, unbuckling my belt.

"Nope," she answers and gets out.

I thought this was going to be a small get together, but clearly I'm wrong. I immediately start looking for Conner. If anyone is going to make me feel comfortable tonight, it's going to be him.

I walk toward the house, glancing back to see the couple I was just talking to still watching me, and, like with most of the other people here, I can't remember their names. I wave at

Skylar, who I'm glad is here, and consider heading in Conner's direction. But he looks deep in conversation with Lucas so I slide the patio door closed behind me and head down the hallway.

I pass two small rooms and a bathroom before I find a room that, I assume by the large desk in the middle, is the den. It has two doors, one that comes from the hallway I am in and one on the other side of the room that leads to the front of the house. I close both doors before sitting on the carpet under the window. Out of sight.

Relationships like the ones I see outside are the type I've wanted my whole life. I came here with the mindset that I would have to work for it and prove myself, but everyone has just accepted me, end of story. They haven't asked questions or pried into my past. Logan, yeah, I expected him to hesitate, but the others … I don't know. Don't they want to know? Do I want them to ask me questions? Maybe, a little.

A part of me wants to ask Logan the questions I wish he'd ask me, but another part of me is scared to hear his answers. What if he grew up with a horrible foster family, or what if he grew up with one that was better than mine? It's not a competition, but I always felt like a piece of my life was missing.

A knock at the door from the hallway takes me from my thoughts. Logan pokes his head inside, his eyes going wide when he sees me.

"Oh, I thought Sara was in here," he says, looking awkwardly around the room. Sorry, brother, nothing to focus on in this room but me.

"Just me," I say.

"Everything okay?"

"Yes."

Now is as good a time as any to change those weird silent moments between us into a real conversation.

"Do you want to join me?" I ask, making the effort we've both been nervous to make. He nods, making his way into the room and looking around, unsure of where he's going to sit. He settles on a spot against the same wall I'm sitting against.

"So, are you doing okay?" he asks. "I mean, how do you like Wind Valley?"

"I'm fine. I like it here. You can thank your best friend for that. He's been amazing since the day I met him. This afternoon, however, with all the people here, is a lot to take in."

Logan tilts his head.

"Yeah, I don't think any of us thought about that when we planned this. We should have though, thought of you." He shakes his head before resting it in his hands, clearly dismissing the subject of Conner.

"It's really okay. I guess I don't know what I was expecting."

"Well, I'll give you a minute or however long you need." He starts to get up.

"No, stay," I blurt out. "I know this whole thing has been a little uneasy for us, but maybe we need baby steps, and staying in a room alone making conversation for longer than five minutes is a good place to start."

He laughs nervously.

"I'm sorry. I've wanted this for so long, and I swear I used to rehearse what I'd say to you, but now that you're here, I'm not sure what to say," he adds, leaning back against the wall.

"I thought about it too."

"About me or about the family we used to have?"

The guilt I used to feel about missing only Logan hits my

heart for a slight moment. Long enough to fear how he might respond to my answer.

"Just you. I don't remember enough about our mother to miss her, and even if I did, she gave up on us. I can't allow myself to care for someone who didn't care for me."

Logan turns his head, and I'm positive I see relief in his eyes.

"Yeah, I feel the exact same way."

We don't say anything else after that. We just sit here for another few minutes, like normal, before Logan excuses himself to get back to his guests. I wait another minute before I come out.

It wasn't anything huge, but knowing we had one feeling alike makes me even happier that I'm here. His opinion means more than it should after not seeing him my whole life.

CHAPTER FIFTEEN

Alexis

The next day, I step into the coffee shop where the entire room smells of fresh, ground brew, which makes my mouth water. I've been craving a caramel macchiato since the day Heather and I bumped into each other.

At three in the afternoon, the place is deserted. I'm the only customer, and after I order my drink it takes only a minute or two until it's ready. I sit by the window, enjoying the view as people walk about the streets. I take another sip of my coffee and watch as an older, gray-haired woman enters the diner across the street that looks similar to the one where I used to work. A mother and her two children, a boy and a girl, are coming around the corner to enter behind the old woman.

Their interaction tugs at my heart. I've always felt like a part of me was missing. I'm not sure if it's because I never got to know my real mother or because I went through multiple foster homes before I found one that accepted me. The one where I met Heather. But I'll always wonder what my life would have been like had I not been in a foster home, and every time I see a little boy and girl, I'll always have this moment of not knowing.

I enjoy the moment where the little boy starts to pester his little sister by pulling on her pigtails. Would Logan and I have acted that way? I played with the other kids in each home and I always had fun, but I'll never know if it would have been more enjoyable if they'd been my real family. Heather was as close as I got to that feeling. She was there when I got my first bra; she taught me how to apply mascara and to not make eyeshadow look like a group of pastel colors threw up on my eyelids. Gosh, Heather was the first person I told about my first crush. I told her everything during our time together. She kept my secrets, the only person I ever talked to when thoughts about my family were on my mind. It's hard to believe we drifted apart all these years, but now we live in the same town, and it makes me feel lighter to have someone from that part of my life around. She'll know what I'm going through.

I hear the squeal of the little girl across the street right before the diner door closes, taking them away from my view.

I pull out my phone in an attempt to distract myself from letting my thoughts of being sad for a part of my life I can't change get too carried away. There isn't any reason for me to dwell on the past. I'm here now, and I have Logan in my life.

I scroll through Facebook and Instagram then I take a snap of myself with puckered lips and crossed eyes and Snapchat it to Conner. He's always sending me random photos of himself during the day. I hope receiving one from me will light up his face with a smile the way mine does.

"Hey, sorry I'm late." Heather comes through the door

looking flustered as she tucks her hair behind her ears and takes off her jacket, hanging it over the back of the chair. "I had to drop my son off with his father."

My eyes go wide.

"You have a little boy?" I ask excitedly as I twist in my seat to face her. She used to go on and on about how she couldn't wait to have a family of her own. Maybe I can have everything I want in my life, too.

"Sure do." She smiles proudly. "I'll tell you all about him after I get some coffee."

She heads for the counter as I turn back to the window. How she's dealing with being a parent, when she grew up the same way I did? I mean, not everyone is going to worry and have the same doubts I do, but I always wonder.

"Okay, so, where should we start?" She takes the seat next to me.

"We can start with how crazy it is that we both ended up in Wind Valley." I laugh.

"Yeah, it's wild. I came here for school but ended up pregnant and alone."

"Alone? What happened to the father?" I didn't realize we were going to jump right into the serious stuff, but, hey, we have a lot to catch up on and we need to start somewhere.

"He wasn't in the right spot in his life to be a father."

"Oh, that's horrible." I cover her hand with my own. "But you managed, right? You're doing okay?"

"Oh, I'm better than okay. My son is just over four years old and is going through a frustrating yet adorable independent phase."

"That's awesome. Has his father tried to be a part of his life?"

"He came back into our lives about two years ago." But her voice changes and she looks away. "That's actually something I want to talk to you about."

"Okay …" Things must not be going as smoothly as I hoped for her. Perhaps we were brought back into each other's lives at the right moment.

"I'm trying to put my relationship with his father back together. You understand more than anyone I know how important family is and how we would do anything to give our children the home life we never had."

"Of course."

"And I want to give my son that chance. To have the family I never got."

"But his father doesn't feel the same?" I ask the question, but I can already tell from the sad tone of her voice what the answer is. "Did he at least tell you why?"

She nods. "He's fallen for someone else and she seems to hold more of his attention than me or our son."

I can't help but roll my eyes. Why a man would choose another woman over his family is something I will never, ever understand. Makes me sick.

"I wish I knew how to help you," I say, leaning back and feeling the sadness radiating off her body.

"Actually, there is something you can do."

I glance at her, my brow rising in interest.

"You can stop seeing Conner."

I blink, not moving any other muscle. I stare with the blankest expression I think my face can make. Everything comes flooding into my mind at once. She wants me to stop seeing Conner. Conner missed out on the first two years of his son's life. Conner is the guy she wants to be with. He's her family. Her son's—their son's—family.

"What, ah … what is, ah …"

"Jake is my son, yes."

One sentence. That's all it takes for my heart to feel as though it's being sliced and gripped and shattered all at once. One sentence is all it takes for me to feel as though I can't breathe.

"I … I …" I can't even form words.

"I'm sorry I just sprang this on you. But I figure if you knew I was trying to put our family back together, you would have stopped anything from starting with Conner. One day he was considering it and the next he changed his mind."

I don't respond to her. My chair screeches as I scoot it away from the counter and grab my purse. I leave her there alone in the coffee shop. I can't do anything right now. I can't believe this is happening. I rush down the street and head for the park, straight for my apartment and Conner's. Only one thing is processing in my mind right now: I cannot and I will never be the reason a child doesn't get his family, and right now, that's exactly who I am.

Conner

Jake sees her first. We're outside, enjoying the sunny, warm weather as he draws with chalk on the sidewalk. Me, I'm drawing too, just not as much. He's mid-draw when he looks up and jumps, squealing.

"Dad! It's Alex! Look!" He points across the street to the park and there she is, walking straight for us. She's walking quickly, which makes me smile. I hate being away from her, too.

"Dad, can she draw with us, please!"

"Yeah, bud, why don't you ask her when she's here?"

"I will." He stands tall and waits for her on the edge of the sidewalk, testing my patience on how close he can get to the road. I start to put some of the broken chalk pieces back in the tub they came in when Jake taps me on the shoulder.

"Dad, Alex is crying," he whispers.

My head snaps back in her direction as I stand. A red and tear-streaked face is watching me as she crosses the street. She doesn't smile at me or even get close enough for me to comfort her. Something isn't right. I swallow, ignoring the terrified pit in my stomach that feels as though I could throw up. Someone hurt her and I want to know who.

"Jake, why don't you go inside?"

"But, Dad, I thought you said I could invite Alex to draw," he whines next to me.

I kneel back down to his height and look him in the eye.

"I need to talk to Alex real fast, okay? We can draw some more when I'm done. Why don't you go see if you can find the neon colors your Uncle E bought for your birthday?" His innocent face lights up and he heads inside the building. When I see his silhouette cross the window of our apartment, I return my focus to Alex.

"What happened?" I ask, taking a slow step forward.

She continues to cry. Each drop of a tear sends a crack to my heart. When I'm close enough to reach her, she takes a step back.

"Don't." Her voice is shaky, but the tone is clear. She doesn't want me to touch her.

"Alex, what happened?"

"All this time," she says, taking a deep breath to control her tears. "All this time you told me you hate secrets. You told me that secrets tear people apart, and you made me feel like I was a horrible person for not telling Logan sooner who I was."

"I did, yes, because it true. Secrets destroy the best things in life."

Apparently those weren't the right words to use. She pins me with a heated glare and storms past me. I grab her arm, stopping her and forcing her to look at me. She turns, jerking her arm out of my hold. That wasn't the right move to make either.

"I'm sorry, I …"

"Sorry for what, Conner? For keeping the biggest secret of all from me? You knew damn well the moment I found out the truth, I'd leave."

She knows about Heather.

"How did you find out?"

"That's all you have to say? Of everything, you're only worried about how I know?" Her fists curl at her sides as she turns once again to head inside. I follow her.

"I wanted to tell you. I wanted to tell you so bad, Alex. I just didn't know how. You expressed how you felt about children not getting the family they deserve, but what good does it do the child if his parents don't love each other? That's not a home life I want Jake to have. Heather and I can't make it work. It has nothing do to with anyone else."

"You should have been the one to tell me." She whips around, surprising me, and I almost run into her. "You, Conner. Not Heather."

I blow out a breath.

"How do you know Heather?"

"Ahhh, really!"

"Okay, yes, it was wrong. I should have told you right away and I didn't, but that doesn't change anything we have."

"It changes everything. We," she points back and forth between us, "have nothing. Whatever this was is over."

"Don't say that. We can figure something out."

"You should at least try to be with her."

"I can't."

"Why not?"

"Because I'm in love with you and not her!"

I stand there, chest heaving as I wait for a response. All I get is more tears before she looks away.

"I'm sorry, Conner. I won't be the reason a family doesn't get their chance."

She closes her door. I step into her doorway, leaning against the frame.

"Alex, please talk to me. I'm sorry."

I wait. But she never answers.

"Dad, is Alex still sad?" Jake asks, appearing in our doorway with his neon chalk. I take the chalk from him as we step outside.

"Yeah, bud, she's still sad."

But he's already too distracted by his own artwork to reply. I'm good with that because I'm sad too. Heartbroken. And I hope Jake never has to experience this feeling in his whole life.

CHAPTER SIXTEEN

Conner

Eating dinner at Heather's place, just me, her, and Jake, isn't what I had planned for this random Thursday evening. But it's been three weeks since Alex and I last spoke, when she told me it was over, and I couldn't stand the thought of her seeing Heather come to my place for dinner. Heather suggested this so we can talk about the next step with Jake. Somewhere in the back of my mind, I know she invited me here to talk about us, and even though my mind is screaming *get out!,* my heart is telling me that maybe if I give it a chance, it will somehow bring Alex back to me in a strange, twisted way. If I become the man she thinks I'm capable of being, maybe she'll change her mind.

"Conner, are you listening to anything I'm saying?"

I hesitate to look at her. I spot Jake instead, playing on the carpet with his plastic Ninja Turtles as he pretends to be Splinter.

"Conner?"

"Hmm?" is my only response. Jake was happy when he was with Alex, too. He likes her. What we had was good for not only me, but him, too. That has to mean something.

"Conner, I swear, you should have a better reaction to this."

"To what?" I ask, finally giving in and joining the discussion she is having.

"To Jake going to school in Wind Valley." By the tone of her voice, I'd say she's annoyed. This, statement, however, brings me a bit of peace.

"That's great, Heather. He's going to love it there."

"I was also thinking it might be a good idea for me find an apartment there. Make it easier on both of us. It would also mean you can see Jake more."

I nod instead of reply.

"I know that things are … uneasy right now. I overstepped my place when I spoke with Alex, but she needed to know."

I eye her, irritated that she brought her up.

"Did she tell you how we met?" Heather knows exactly how to get my attention. Apparently she wants all of it instead of letting me watch my son play on his own. Alex used to play with him. She always played Donatello and Jake loved it.

"No, we never got that far," I answer.

"My last foster home was the same as hers, and we lost touch when I left."

"And you decided now was the time to come back into her life."

"No, I didn't know she worked at the gym until I ran into her and then I put a few things together. She has strong feelings toward family …"

"I know all this. I know her better than you do. I want to

be in her life because I love her, not because we share a past that you clearly didn't care about. If you had, you would have stayed in touch."

"She wants you to give Jake a chance …"

"Do not say it. I've heard it a million times, Heather. And I don't know what I have to say or do to get it through your head or hers that without love, you and I will never work."

"You could love me though, one day, right?" Her voice is in pieces.

"I'm sorry, Heather."

She nods, excusing herself from the table. I gather Jake's things and we head home. I'm the bad guy no matter where I go. Call me a sap or call me whipped, but I want to end up with the woman I love. I just need to figure out how to make her see it.

Alexis

Logan is upset with Conner, and I feel guilty enjoying what it feels like to have an overprotective brother. Ever since I told Sara what happened she's invited me around more. I honestly think she would have even if Conner and I were still together. Seeing as how he lives across from me and comes into the gym almost every night I work, the distraction has been nice.

"Did he knock on your door today?" Logan asks as he takes a seat on his sofa between Sara and Beth. We were going to have a girl's lunch, but Kelsey wasn't feeling up to it. I don't blame her, considering her due date was yesterday.

"He did." The same way he has every day since I broke things off between us.

"And you still didn't answer?" Beth asks.

"What am I going to say to him, honestly?"

"Honestly," Logan clears his throat. "It's not your choice to make for him. If he wants to be with you rather than her, then let it happen."

"Logan!" Sara exclaims. "I thought you were against them being together."

He shrugs and pulls out his phone. "I used to feel that way. And mainly because I didn't want Alex to get hurt. I always wanted her to be happy, though."

"I agree with Logan," Beth says.

I eye each of them as I decide what I want to say. Whether or not I want to, it seems like I'm doing something wrong if I forgive him so easily.

"Look, I know how it sounds, and yeah, I'm sure I'm one of the last people you would want to be taking advice from, but you have to go with the flow," Logan says, surprising me.

"Seriously, that's your big brother advice? You've waited this many years to tell her that?" Sara rolls her eyes but is smiling at the same time.

"No, I've waited this many years to see my sister living a life where she is happy and has what she wants. What I see: messy hair, jeans, and hoodie. This doesn't look like you're happy."

I sigh. He's right. I'm not happy, but I can't take back what I said and I don't want to. I refuse to be the other woman. And I might not even be that. But it doesn't change the fact that Conner kept Heather and her suggestion they be a family from me. He had plenty of moments to tell me about it and explain his side of the story, but he never did. It stings to think that maybe he never said a word because he doesn't trust me. Or maybe he wasn't really as into me as I was him. Maybe I was just someone to help pass the time or get out one last hurrah before he made the family commitment.

"If you ask me, I think you two just need to talk it out." Sara grins at me before she reaches over to rub Logan's back. The way she looks at Logan, with love, hits me right in the heart. I don't think I was ever in love with Conner, but it was something fiercely close.

"Do you remember how you lacked a lot of communication? Maybe it's something that runs in the family," Sara says.

"It's not the lack of communication as much as we don't want to face the fact that someone might not want us, would reject us the way our parents did," Logan says with such a straight face. Then he kisses his wife on the top of her head and stands. "I've voiced my opinion. I'll let you ladies talk it out from here. But, Alexis, I'm serious. When you fall in love, you can't control what it does to you. How it makes you feel. You should embrace it. Conner isn't leaving Jake behind by being with you. He's still being the father we never had with or without you. I have a feeling he'd rather do it with you."

I open my mouth, but to say what I'm not sure. I'm starting to think that Logan hogged all the smart genes when he was born. He winks at Sara before he exits the room. His experience is what has made him so wise. I hope mine will do the same.

"Personally, I think—" Beth begins but is cut off by Logan barging back into the room.

"Kelsey is having the baby!"

"What?" Sara says with excitement.

"Finally." Beth says.

"Ethan says it's going fast; let's go." Logan grabs his keys and Sara's purse from near the door.

"Why do we need to be there?" I ask, not moving from the couch.

All three of them pause to stare at me.

"Why wouldn't we go? Our best friend is having a baby and we want to be there for her. This is what we do. This is how our group works. Now I know you like Kelsey, too, so if you're part of our group then you best get your ass off that couch and suck up the nerves or whatever else you are going to have when you see Conner." Beth barely finishes her mini speech before she's out the door. Sara, who is just starting her fifth month, is right behind her.

Beth is right. All of these people have welcomed me into their lives even after knowing I kept my relation to Logan a secret. They didn't hesitate to make me feel like I've found more than just friends. This is my new family—they were there for me and now it's my turn to repay the favor.

I stand.

Twenty minutes later I'm sitting in the hospital waiting room with Beth, Sara, Logan, and Kelsey's parents. Clara is fast asleep in her grandmother's arms. I want to ask where Ethan's parents are, but no one seems to be concerned about it, so I decide it's best not to bring it up. I expected Conner to be here already, but he isn't. I really want to ask about that because a part of me is actually looking forward to seeing him. I miss his touch and the way he gives me this half grin thing that creates one dimple on the right side of his smile just before he kisses me.

I lean back in my chair the moment I hear Jake. He zooms into the room and right to his grandparents. Who, I might add, have had the biggest smiles I've ever seen on their faces. Today is happy day for them, too.

"Alex!" he yells the moment his eyes catch mine over his grandfather's shoulder mid hug. Jake scrambles down to his feet and runs over to me, wrapping his arms around my neck as I lean over the chair into his embrace.

"Dad said you've been real busy this week. So busy you can't even play chalk with me." Big, sad eyes look up at me. I see Conner in them and it crushes my heart even more.

"Yeah, I have. But how about next time you're staying at your dad's, I'll meet you outside for a chalk date."

"Yes! Dad, did you hear her?"

My gaze remains glued to the floor as I feel Conner looking at me. If I look up, I can't promise I won't break into tears. I don't know what has gotten into me. I've only known him a few months. This shouldn't be the way I feel after such a short amount of time.

"Yeah, I heard her, bud." His voice sends welcomed shivers through my body, waking parts of me that have a desire only for him. His arm brushes against mine as he takes the seat next to me. Jake is now chatting Sara and Logan's ears off on the other side of the room.

"I've been trying to talk to you," he says quietly.

"I know."

"Can you give me the chance to explain myself? I never thought I would meet someone like you, and everything got complicated so fast. I was so caught up in what we had that I got scared."

"Conner, I don't think this is the place to talk."

"I disagree. I told myself that the next time I saw you, I wouldn't waste another minute missing my chance to talk to you. Waiting for the right moment is what put me in this spot to begin with. I miss you, Alex. And I'm so incredibly sorry."

"Conner, please," I beg, swiping a tear away. These rushes of emotions are new for me and I don't really feel like crying in public.

"Alex, I can't be with her when I'm in love with you."

I rise, ready to dash out of the room when Ethan steps in, smiling like a proud new father.

"Kelsey is doing great and out newest addition, Cassie, is just as beautiful as her mother. You should be able to see her soon."

Everyone takes their turn giving hugs and congratulating him. I do my part and excuse myself.

I can't stick around here. Not while Conner is here, and not while my heart shatters just by looking at him.

CHAPTER SEVENTEEN

Conner

Two weeks. That's how long it's been since I saw Alex in the hospital and that's how long she's been avoiding me. My sister Kelsey, Beth, and Sara all said to give her space and she will come around. I've been doing my best, but right now, I really wish I hadn't listened to them. I don't think she needs more time.

She's going on a date. I saw him walk up to the building with flowers in hand. At first I hoped it was the grandson of the woman who lives above me, but when I hear her laugh coming from the hall I know what's going on. I don't like it at all.

I swing my door open just as Alex is locking hers.

"Hey there," I say to the guy, who is staring at her ass. I lean against my doorframe and smile when she turns around with a warning written all over her face. I can't really confirm what kind of warning it is though; it almost looks as though she's trying not to smile. Then her date turns to look at me, too, and I push off the wall. Fucking Pete.

"Where are you two headed?" I ask, flashing her the grin I know she loves.

"That's none of your business," she says, stepping toward the door. I take a step, too, stopping in front of her to block her from leaving.

"As your neighbor, I'm looking out for you. Plus, Logan may have asked me to keep an eye on you."

"He did not." She rolls her eyes.

"Maybe, but then again, no one needs to ask me to make sure you stay safe."

"I'm sorry," Pete interrupts. "Did you two spilt up, or is there still something going on?"

"He's just my neighbor."

"Ouch." I put my hand over my heart for fun. "I may be her ex, but I guarantee you won't get far enough to get even that title."

Pete's eyes go wide.

"Correction, you were never my boyfriend. A relationship with titles requires trust. Something you were clearly lacking." She moves for the door and I stop her, again.

"I hate that our relationship is still raw on your heart, and if I remember right, you kept something from me too."

Her eyes lock onto mine and we're suddenly in a staring contest.

"Maybe I should go?" Pete asks.

"No, Pete, Conner is going back inside his apartment so we can go on our date."

"I was actually thinking of seeing you off. You know, make sure Pete is being a true gentleman."

"Look, Conner, I've seen your type before, and guess what? You don't get the girl in the end." Pete takes a step toward me, but I'm still a good head taller than him.

"That may be true, but I also know that she isn't into people claiming her the way you're trying to right now," I say.

"Conner, seriously." Alex's annoyed tone does nothing but make me feel triumphant. I wanted to affect her and I did. She'll be back later tonight. Probably to yell at me, but I'll smooth talk her down.

What am I saying? I'm desperate. I'll do anything to get her to talk to me, including making things worse.

I lift my hand and back away in surrender form.

"Sure, by all means, go on your date."

Pete bumps me with his shoulder as he passes through the door. I have to take a deep breath to keep myself from sending him off with a black eye. He doesn't know how lucky he is to be going out with her right now.

With Pete through the door, I gently grab Alex's arm before she can follow him. This time she doesn't look like she's ready to rip my head off.. Her eyes appear on the verge of tears as they avoid looking directly at mine.

"No amount of time is going to change the way I feel about you. No guy is going to come in here, take you out, and push me away. You're it for me, and I'll wait as long as it takes until you figure that out."

I kiss her forehead and she sighs before rushing out the door. What else can I do to make her see we are meant to be together?

I watch as Pete's car pulls away from the curb. I must zone out because the next thing I notice is that same car parking in front of the BA. I'm out the door and headed that way in under a minute.

Alexis

I wonder if Pete knows Conner works at the BA. If he does then he's an idiot, and if he doesn't, I feel bad for the guy because I have a good feeling no matter who is working, they won't be that pleasant to him. I know this because for the last week I've heard how cruel I'm being by not listening to what Conner has to say and that I'm being dumb—Beth's exact word—to not give him another chance.

Falling in love is supposed to be easy. It shouldn't come with secrets and problems right off the bat, and because that's exactly what happened with us, it couldn't have been real love.

Although he sure seems convinced it is, and his words tonight still affect me the way they did the first time he said them.

"Have you ever been here?" Pete asks as he opens a menu. I open mine, too, avoiding Lucas's stare from behind the bar.

I should probably spare Pete the details—this is the exact booth where my story with Conner began. He's all I can think about, but I'm positive he's the last thing Pete wants to talk about.

"My brother and sister-in-law actually own this bar, so I've been here before, yes."

"Oh, you should have said something. We can go somewhere else if you want."

"No, the food here is great."

Pete eyes me then with a blank expression. I force a smile.

"Hello, Alexis, and hello, Pete." Of course, Abby would be the only cheery person to wait on us tonight. I don't miss the way she gets all excited to see Conner at the gym. And I sure don't miss the way she finds excuses to be in the same area he is.

I narrow my eyes, hating how jealous I am, because I shouldn't be jealous. There isn't and won't be an Alexis and Conner.

I'm about to order my entire dinner so I can get this date over with—I'm only here to prove to Beth that I'm over Conner—when the guy himself walks through the door. He looks great in his dark wash jeans and gray hoodie. Sad eyes meet mine, and it forces me to look away for a brief moment.

Pete groans at the sight of him and Abby excuses herself, letting us know she'll be back with two waters. Conner keeps his eyes on our table as he moves toward the bar.

"He's not seriously following you, is he?"

"No, he works here. He's not crazy." I'm suddenly defensive.

Pete glares at me so I glare back.

"You know what, I'm going to head out. Think your boyfriend can give you a ride?" he says sarcastically, rising from the table.

"I'll walk since you drove me a whole block."

Pete lets out a grunt laugh and leaves me sitting at the table alone. Well, work will be fun next week.

I continue to sit there when Abby brings me a water, and I decline her offer to get me some food.

Alright, so maybe everyone else is right. Even Logan told me I need to let go of the past, that nothing that happened before I got here should affect where I end up. Maybe I should just talk to Conner, but like everything else in my life, I need the time to do it on my own.

"This seat taken?" Conner asks, not waiting for an answer before he sits down. I take a deep breath and look up. It takes everything I have not to start crying.

"You know just as well I as I do that we are meant to be together. You're just wasting your time dating other guys," he says. He doesn't say it like he's mad, he says it like he understands why I'm doing it. His voice is calm and soft and it makes me want to both scream and cry that he thinks me knows me as well as he does.

"No, I don't know that," I snap and head for the door. He calls my name, but I don't stop. I even make it all the way home before it occurs to me that he didn't come after me and it frustrates me because I wanted him to.

I'm a mess.

CHAPTER EIGHTEEN

Conner

There was a moment last night when I thought I was getting through to her. Instead I made matters worse. Maybe she doesn't feel like I do. Maybe it really is over.

Jake stirs next to me on the couch. The poor kid was dropped off by his mother once again for a reason she can't explain. Like a couple of times before, she was crying when she left.

She wouldn't tell me why.

Things were great and now I feel like I can't get any part of my life together. With Jake in my arms, I walk to his room and lay him onto his bed before reaching for his backpack to grab his pajamas. It's almost time to get him a bigger bed. This kid is growing up too fast for me.

I pull a pair of dinosaur pajamas from the big pocket and a white envelope falls out. Seeing it on my floor with my name written across the front sends a sinking feeling to my gut.

I finish changing Jake and tuck him in before I pull out the letter. The first two words force me to the edge of the bed before I make it out of the room.

I'm sorry, Conner.

I won't be picking Jake up this time around. I've been doing this mom thing for a while now and it's not working out for me. I can't do it. Not alone, and I can't force you to be with me at all times. I knew the idea was absurd the moment I mentioned it.

This is a selfish choice. I know it. But I've been thinking about it for a while now and Jake will be better off without me.

The last few months when Jake comes back to me after spending time with you and Alexis, the smile on his face is brighter than any day he's with me. He's always talking about you and your family, and until recently he'd always speak of Alexis. He's very fond of her. Maybe the reason I met her when I was younger and confided in her all those years ago was because Fate knew she would one day raise my son. He's in good hands with you and with her. He will be truly happy with the both of you.

I'm not sorry I held such high standards for you. For making you get your own place, go back to school, and get a steady job. I knew this day would come and I wanted to make sure Jake was going to be safe and well cared for before I left him. I knew you could give him so much more than I ever could on my own.

I know this doesn't make sense to you, but this has been my plan from the day I told you that you are a father. If I couldn't make us a family, I knew I wouldn't be able to stick around. I'm not a good mom for him.

The hate you feel for me right for giving up on Jake is something I will never ask you to forgive me for. I promise I won't be coming back into your life years later to take him from you. To prove this to you, I've enclosed adoption papers. My signature is already on them. If Alexis wants to become his legal mother, I know she will give Jake the world because she is a much stronger person than I am. I hope I didn't ruin things between you two permanently. If you're not back together yet, try harder. Try harder than I ever did to be a mother.

I'll always love my son, but his life will be so rich with you.

Heather

Tears are in my eyes before I can finish reading. Not for me, or for the way my life is going to be different from this moment on, but for my son whose mother is giving up. For the kid who has been through enough this past year and doesn't deserve this. I glance back at his unaware and innocently sleeping face.

How could his mother do this to him?

I flick the light off as I exit his room. Everything is about to change, and out of all the people I have right now that I can call, the one person I want it to be still isn't speaking to me.

. . .

Alexis

He's right there. Just across the hall. Ten steps, maximum. All I have to do is walk out my door, knock on his, and tell him I'm sorry and I'm wrong. My hand rests above the doorknob; I can't decide what to do.

I know this is what I want to do and that it's what I need to do, yet somehow I can't do it. Something keeps telling me today isn't a good day to tell him. Another part of me keeps reminding myself that if I don't suck it up and do it right now, I may lose my chance, or worse, convince myself yet again to do the wrong thing. I don't want either of those.

With a deep breath in and out, I turn the knob. Conner steps out of his apartment the same moment, holding Jake's backpack in his hand. I've noticed that Jake has been here the last few days. The look of frustration on Conner's face and the circles under his eyes go straight to my heart. I want to hold him, tell him how sorry I am, and offer to help with whatever he has going on. My not knowing what I want has affected him more deeply than I thought. I hope I'm not too late.

I stand there, waiting for him to say something as we stare at each other. He doesn't though, and his phone interrupts whatever moment we were having. His eyes widen and he quickly moves to grab it, switching Jake's backpack to the other hand as he answers.

"I'm on my way, I swear it," he says, not waiting for a reply and placing the phone back into his jeans. "Jake, let's go," he hollers into the apartment.

"Is everything okay?" I ask. He's more flustered than usual, and it's selfish of me to assume that his appearance is solely because of me.

"No, we're just running late," he answers softly, glancing

back into his apartment. He then drops the backpack and steps back through the door, leaving it wide open. I step toward it.

"Jake, what are you doing?" I hear him ask.

"I can't find Donny," Jake's small voice answers in a panic.

"We can find him later," Conner says.

"Noooo," Jakes cries out. "We have to find him now."

I hear Conner's aggravated sigh, followed by the sounds of Jake's toy buckets being moved around. "Where did you last have it?"

Their conversation grows louder as I step inside to help. When Jake napped, he would always leave Donny under the blanket he used on the couch. I lift the same brown and gold tie blanket he always uses and, sure enough, the stuffed green turtle is resting right underneath it.

"He's right here," I call out to them and Jake comes running, pure excitement on his face as he rounds the corner into the living room.

"Alex!" he screams and crashes into my legs, hugging them tightly. I smile and bend over, doing my best to hug him back.

"Thank you," Conner's voice catches my attention. He's standing right in front of me. My eyes lock with his for a brief moment before he squats to help Jake tie his shoes.

"I don't want this to come off as rude, but Jake and I are sort of in a hurry, so—"

"Oh yeah, it's not a problem." I turn for the door.

"Are you coming back tonight?" Jake asks, looking down to line up the zipper on his jacket.

"I'm sure she has other things to do, bud," Conner answers for me, and that's when it occurs to me that I'm too late. He didn't look at me with hopeful eyes or ask me himself. He just dismissed it like he doesn't care to hear what I had to say. Which is fair; it's what I've been doing to him the last few weeks.

I nod, forcing a smile over the tears that want to fall.

We all step through the door and Jake grabs his backpack.

"I go to Nanna's now while Dad is working. It's part of our new team."

"Routine," Conner says. "Not new team."

"Oh yeah, that." Jake smiles, rolls his eyes, and is out the door.

I want to ask Conner more, but he follows Jake outside without another word. I close the door behind me and sink to the floor. The tears come uncontrollably as I face the facts: I ruined everything we had.

Work is slow when I make it to the gym later. Slow sucks because that means I have more time to let my mind dwell on everything I could have done differently.

I walk by the windows in the cardio room, noticing the rain has picked up, turning what was a bright and sunny day into a gloomy one. It's like my life right now. I had hope this morning and now I just feel out of sorts. Great, what's next? The treadmill represents the never-ending road of sadness that lies ahead?

Yeah, I need to get out of this area.

At the front desk, Abby is folding towels. I join her, not saying a word. If anyone has enjoyed what's going on between me and Conner, it's her.

I'm two towels in and she sighs. I ignore it. Another towel later, she sighs again, this time louder.

"What?" I ask, irritated.

"Oh, nothing."

"Clearly it's something," I say. She better spit it out before I snap and say something I could regret later after I've been fired.

"Alright, but it has more to do with you than me," she says, continuing to fold. Me, however, I've got my arms crossed and my hip resting against the counter as I look at her.

"I'm the reason you're sighing rudely?"

"Rudely? I needed a reason to get you to talk to me because you haven't said one word to me since you got here."

"Didn't know it was part of my job."

"Fine, I know I'm not your favorite person and you won't like what I'm about to say, but you need to hear me out."

"I don't have to do anything."

"Please." Her voice changes to one of pleading and the look in her eyes is actually sincere.

"Fine."

"You know my past and you know how I feel about Conner." I turn to leave, but she grabs my arm. "But," she practically yells, "I also know him well enough to know that he's in love with you, not me. That the only person he wants is you, not me. And that the only person he needs right now is you, not me."

I swallow back even more tears and avoid looking at her. She didn't see him dismiss me today. I should tell her that she's wrong, because he clearly doesn't want me anymore, but I'm not ready to accept it yet and I sure don't want her thinking that in time she can swoop in and be the woman he needs.

"You may not believe me, but I work with him, too, you know. The two of you are acting in the exact depressed, life-is-over way, and if working two jobs isn't bad enough, having people around to bum me out makes it even worse."

"I'm not depressed," I say, making a sad attempt to disagree with her.

"*You* are and *he* is, so do something about it. And do it soon because the chance to be happy and in love doesn't just happen to anyone."

I let her words sink in. Is she talking about herself? Is that why she wants what she can't have, because she wants to be happy and in love? She resumes folding without looking at me again. I watch her for good minute, waiting for an action or facial expression to give me more of an idea what she's thinking. She doesn't give anything away so I grab another towel.

"Thank you" is all I say, and that's the last we talk about me and Conner for the night.

To be happy and in love.

Conner didn't give up after one attempt to talk to me and I shouldn't either. When I get home tonight, I'm going to his apartment to demand we have a real conversation. And if that doesn't work, I'll go to him every day until he figures it out, just like he did all those times with me. I love him, too, and it's about time he knew.

CHAPTER NINETEEN

Conner

All evening I've been watching The Weather Channel. It's been a downpour since the moment I left for work. Driving to pick up Jake after my shift—I worked the early one—the rain beating against the window made it hard to see. Now it's just after ten at night, dark, and the roads are more than likely slick with the drop in temperature. Alex still isn't home.

I'm not a stalker, but my feelings for her won't go away in a day and I don't like the idea of her driving in this weather. When we were together it was easy to figure out her schedule, and I know for a fact that she should have been home ten minutes ago from work. It's possible she could have plans after work, but if I know Alex at all, on a night like this she would cancel. She's a smart woman.

I flick back the curtains in the living room once more, peeking up and down the street in search for any headlights. Nothing.

Earlier, when I saw her in the hallway, I wanted to believe

she was out there because she was finally coming to me. But she never said anything. When Jake invited her over, I wanted to join him and beg her to listen to me or even just be in the same room. Instead, I gave her an easy out. She hasn't wanted to be around me since she found out about Heather being Jake's mom; I wasn't about to trick her by using my son. That, and now that Heather isn't in the picture, I'm a package deal with Jake. My heart aches knowing Alex is the one person who wouldn't give that idea a second thought.

The couch swallows up my son's small body. He's sound asleep with not a care in the world. I haven't told him about his mom yet. He thinks she's on a vacation again. I'll have to tell him the truth sooner rather than later, but each time I think this is it, this is the moment to tell him, my heart breaks. He's too young to feel this pain, and I hate his mother more and more every day because she's making him go through this.

The sound of a car driving by and splashing water makes me return to the window. It's still not Alex. Something isn't right.

I wrap Jake in a blanket and carry him to my truck. He wakes for just a moment at the cold touch of the rain, but once he's buckled in his seat, he's fast asleep.

The gym isn't too far from our apartment. If she crashed or ran off the road for whatever reason, I won't miss it.

I drive slowly, my windshield wipers flapping fast, trying to give me a clear view. It only takes me a couple blocks before I see her. Her car is pulled to the side with the hazard lights on. When I pull up in front of her, I see her small figure drenched in a hoodie as she tries to change her tire.

Leaving the truck running, I jump out and jog to her.

"Alex, what are you doing?" I ask even though it's clear I

know what she's doing, but I don't understand why she didn't just call me or come home and return to this later.

"I'm changing my tire." She sniffles. "What does it look like?"

"I see that, but come on." I take off my jacket and hold it over our heads as I crouch down next to her. "Let's go home and fix this in the morning."

"I can do it." She sniffles again, and I recognize the noise as something not due from the cold and a runny nose, but because she's crying.

"Alex," I say calmly.

"No, I'm fine—just go. I'm going to do it tonight."

"Alex," I say again, this time reaching out to gently grab her chin and force her to look at me. It takes a moment before her eyes look up. "Let's go home."

"I can't."

"Why not?"

"Because nothing else was supposed to get in the way of us being together. You being in a hurry this morning was a sign, and now me getting a flat after I told myself the first thing I was doing after work was coming to talk to you is another sign that we aren't supposed to talk. That this isn't going to ever work."

"By this, do you mean us?" I ask just to be clear.

"Yes, we aren't meant to be." She starts to sob, falling into my shoulder as she cries.

I want to ask what she was coming to me to talk about, but I don't want to make things worse than the way she sees them right now. Tonight, I'm not letting her go until we are back together.

"I see it differently," I begin, wishing we could have this

conversation in my truck where it's dry. "I think you were meant to get a flat so you would have to come to me sooner. So you had no choice to back out."

"What?" She pushes away to look at me.

"Yeah, I think your life wasn't about to let you go another day without me, so to prove it, it decided to remind you how much you need me."

She blinks, wipes away the mixture of rain and tears, and then laughs. The sound warms my entire soul. I thought I'd never see that smile again.

"Your version of my flat tire is so much better than mine. That right there is why I love you," she says and my heart stops.

"You love me?"

She nods, biting her bottom lip. "I should have told you a long time ago."

I don't know if she planned to say anything else, but I don't let her. My lips steal any words she was about to say. I kiss her hard, never letting our lips part as we stand. When we finally pull away, I wrap her in my coat and I hold her tightly. There is no way I'm ever letting her go again.

EPILOGUE

Alexis

The last couple months have been better than I ever imagined they could be. I glance over in the waiting room to see Jake laying on one of the chairs with his head in Conner's lap. Conner's head is tipped back and his eyes are closed. Yes, it's late, and yes, I should be sleeping, too, but I'm too excited to sleep. Any minute now I'm going to be an aunt. The black coffee I'm sipping on is also helping. I don't want to be asleep when Logan finally comes out.

The silence the waiting room brings to me allows me to reflect on how my life has changed in the last six months. I moved to a new town, have a relationship with my brother, met a guy and fell in love with both him and his son, I have the best of friends, and I'm happier than I ever thought possible.

We don't have any more secrets. Conner told me about Heather right after we got home that rainy night. The night he told Jake about his mother has been the only heartbreaking moment since Conner and I got back together. Jake didn't cry and he didn't ask anything other than if I or his dad was going anywhere, but I wanted to cry for him. I saw relief in his eyes when we said we were sticking around. We'll never know what his life was like when he was with Heather, but we do know that his life will be the best now because he has me and the best father a kid could ask for.

Jake stirs and his foot stretches out to kick over Conner's backpack, knocking a book onto the floor.

I moved into Conner's apartment just before the fall semester started and I switched to just days at work. At night, while Conner is either at the BA or taking night classes at the local college, I watch Jake.

Of course, Logan complained about us rushing things, but we ignored him because we knew it was right. He still acts weird about the whole Conner and me thing, but honestly, I think he loves it. He just won't admit it.

"Hey, what time is it?" Conner whispers.

I glance at my cell phone.

"Just after midnight," I answer.

Her rubs his sleepy eyes and flashes me a grin. It's the same grin that make me blush every time he looks in my direction. Even now. I lean over the small table between us and kiss him.

"Seriously? Every time I see the two of you, you're kissing. Do you know where that leads you? Right here, that's where." Logan's father voice is spot on. "It's a boy," he adds proudly.

Another hour later, with Jake now lying in a chair in Sara's room, I get to meet the newest addition to my family.

"I can't believe I'm an aunt," I whisper to Conner as he

stands behind me and we gaze down at my nephew, Brock. He's sleeping in his blue swaddled blanket in his spot next to Sara's bed. She, too, is sleeping, or pretending, I'm not sure. I don't blame them. They both had a rough night.

"It's a crazy feeling, huh?" Conner kisses just below my ear as he wraps his arms around my mid-section and rests his chin on my shoulder. "Almost feels unreal that you can love someone so much, doesn't it?"

I nod.

"Just wait until we have kids. The feeling is multiplied by like a million."

"Oh, we're having kids?"

"Someday, yeah." I feel his cheek press against mine as he smiles.

"Can I see?" Jake comes up behind me, his lips forming an o shape as Conner picks him up so he can see baby Brock. I hadn't even realized he woke up, but he's in this sneaking around the apartment phase. He also enjoys scaring me. I hate it, but he's so cute when he does it.

"Well, aren't you the cutest little family," Logan says from the doorway.

"Congrats again," Conner says, shaking Logan's hand and patting him on the shoulder. "You're lucky he's a cute little thing and got all of Sara's looks."

"Ha ha, funny."

"I'm serious though, you've got a beautiful family right here," Conner says, giving Logan a shoulder squeeze.

"I should be saying the same thing to you." Logan grins at him. "I never did officially tell you how I happy I am you're the guy my sister ended up with."

This earns him a hug from both me and Conner.

As I stand there, wrapped in the arms of my brother and the man I love, I know life can only get better from here.

The day I met Conner was the day my heart was touched and recharged. Moving to Wind Valley and meeting him changed my entire life, and even after everything that's happened in my past, I wouldn't change a thing if it means I end up here. This is where I'm meant to be.

***

Want more from Jami?
Subscribe to her mailing list for exclusive bonus epilogues
and all the book news!

Ready for Luke's story?
Start reading Just One Moment today!

JUST ONE MOMENT
CHAPTER ONE

Luke

The urge to shout "fuck it" is at the tip of my tongue at least once a day.

I never actually say it, though. All it would cause is a whole lot more pain in my mother's heart. I'd rather claw my eyes from their sockets than ever witness my mother shed another tear.

I'd do anything for my family. Even it if means stopping by my mom's house in between jobs to make sure she and my sisters are doing alright. I really should be using this hour to either relax, because working two jobs—one that I am part owner in—and being a full-time art major student is exhausting. Or I should study for an exam I have coming up next week to end the summer semester. I'll be the first to admit it that "free time" isn't part of my vocabulary these days, but I struggle to choose which is more important: living the life I want or making sure my family has the life they deserve.

I park my 1968 Dodge Charger RT on the curb outside my

mother's house and head inside. A chirp sounds behind me as I press the lock button and stuff the keys into my pocket. Its bright, cherry-apple red stands out in her old, dingy neighborhood.

Mom's new neighbors stay up late playing loud music, random cars are always coming and going, and they use their front yard as a trash can. Not to mention the excessive amount of arguing that happens in the middle night. I hate to judge, but the idea of my family living near these people worries me, and I'm pretty convinced that it's drug deal behavior at the house on their left. Locking my car is a must. Especially when building this car back to life was the last thing my father and I did together. It's my last memory with him, and I'll never let it go.

"Lucas."

My mother, Julianne Warren, greets me in her soft, warm tone as I step through the door. I give her a full, tight hug—the way I always do when I see her—and she smiles up at me. It's her normal smile, but there's still a light shade under eyes. *I hope she starts sleeping better soon.*

"How many times do I have to tell you that you do not have to check up on me?"

She can tell me as much as she wants, but I'll never listen. Ever since my dad passed away, things have been hard on all of us. Between working extra shifts at the hospital, making sure twin thirteen-year-old girls have rides where they need to be, food to eat, and still being a mom who's actively in their lives for sports and whatever else they do, Mom has it the worst of all. She pretends it doesn't take a toll on her and my sisters, but I can see it in the way her eyes wrinkle at the crease more each time I visit.

"I have no idea what you're talking about," I tell her, grinning because it's how I reply every time. She swats at my arm and rolls her eyes. "You act just like your father."

She laughs and heads for the dining room. "Your sisters are in the living room. Don't get them all wound up before you leave."

This time it's my turn to laugh. "I never do that. Those two feed off each other."

"Yeah, okay," she says, her dark hair swooshing to the side as she disappears through the entry into the kitchen.

I toe off my shoes and hang my coat on a free peg by the door. It's a wooden coat rack that my dad made when I was seven. There are two pegs lying on the floor. How three women can break those off I have no idea, but I make a mental note to fix it later.

I step quietly into the living room and spy Brandy sprawled out on the couch with her phone in her hands and Shea sitting on the floor with her back against the couch as she reads from the book clenched between her fingers. They both have rich brown hair that falls to the middle of their backs, bright green eyes, and freckles that sprinkle just over their noses. If it weren't for the fact that Shea prefers her glasses to contacts, people would never be able to tell them apart. It amazes me how much they look like our mother. I have the same dark hair, only buzzed short, and I have blue eyes, like my dad.

I can't believe how much they're growing up. These next few years are going to be some wild ones for Mom.

"I'm actually impressed the TV isn't on right now," I say.

"Luke!" Brandy cheers and jumps off the couch to hug me. "I was hoping you'd stop by. I have a question for you."

"Don't you even dare ask him!" Shea looks up from her book, glaring at Brandy. It's definitely a look that would make me think twice.

"Well, he is a guy, Shea. He'll probably have some great advice."

Oh no.

"Shea likes a boy, but she doesn't know how to get his attention. I told her to just go up to him and say hey, and if he walks away then move on to the next one."

Move on to the next one?

"Tell me once when that advice has worked for you," Shea snaps.

I sit on the back of the couch as both girls are now standing in front of me with their hands on their hips as they face each other. Mom must be loving these new teen years.

"Considering guys have never walked away from me, I'm certain it will work," Brandy says.

What the?

"Whoa," I say, shaking my head and holding my hands up. "I do have advice." They both direct their bodies toward me and cross their arms. I look them both in the eyes before I continue. "Neither of you should be thinking of anything that involves boys."

"Oh, come on, Luke, we're thirteen now. It's totally normal," Shea says.

"Yea, I mean I've already been kissed. This is just the first—"

"Mom!" I yell, cutting Brandy off. No way I'm going to let her finish that sentence. Who cares that I'm twenty-four years old and hollering for my mother like a kid.

"Why are you yelling?" Mom asks, holding a pan and towel in her hands as she dries.

"Um, because Brandy and Shea are going to be home-schooled from now on," I answer.

"Seriously!"

"Men!"

I'm not sure who said what as they walk away from me to resume their previous spots, but I don't like the tone from either of them. Mom just laughs.

"Come help me with these dishes. I know you're headed somewhere, so you better get in here quick."

Anything is better than listening to my baby sisters' talk about boys and kissing. As much as I hated being an only child and loved it when my parents announced the "oops twins," I do not enjoy moments like that one.

I'm about to cross through the doorway to the kitchen when the last family photo we took with Dad catches my eye. His hand was over my shoulder, and I rub that same spot automatically. That was my first day of freshman year. Everyone had to wait more than an hour for me that day. Mom was upset when I did arrive with paint all over my arms and face, and my family had to wait for me to scrub it off. Dad said if holding me down himself was how they'd get the picture, that was what he would do. That was also the moment Dad reminded me how strong he was.

"Can you believe it's already been more than a year?" Mom whispers to me. Her eyes find mine, and I don't miss the flicker of her gaze from me to my sisters before she nudges me into the kitchen.

"Their school is hosting a father-daughter dance at the

start of this next year. Shea isn't handling it very well, and Brandy is pretending it doesn't bother her."

Of course this would happen just when things were starting to be normal again and not everything they saw reminded them of Dad. I have to look away from Mom; I can see the glaze in her eyes already.

"What if …"

My words trail off. Mom is slowly sliding something under the computer sitting on the table. Bold red capital letters that say "final notice" on not only one but two pieces of mail are peeking out from under her fingers. "What's this? What happened to the money I gave you last week?" I ask, my hands gripping the back of a chair as I lean forward, waiting for her answer. She hesitates and then takes a seat.

"The girls want to be more involved with school and academics this year, but prices have gone up."

My teeth grind together as I take a breath. "Then I'll bring you more money."

"No, Luke, you've done so much this last year. I can't let you sacrifice any more of your life on us."

If Dad's life insurance had covered more than their debt, the Warren woman would be just fine. But it didn't, and I won't let them struggle.

"I'm a grown man, Mom, and I am going to take care of my mother and sisters." I step forward to kiss the top of her head. "I have to get to work, but I'll be back tomorrow."

She doesn't say anything as I walk away, which is good. I don't want to argue with her today. It also saves me from not having to discuss the reason I came here in the first place. The one thing I have been dreading for the last few weeks.

It's time we sell the bookstore. My father's store.

. . .

Skylar

Being homeless is exhausting.

I push against the glass door of the motel's entrance where I've been staying the last week. Chu is working behind the receptionist desk, like he always is. He doesn't stand very tall, and his eyes can barely see over the top of the wooden counter as he watches me step inside. His black hair is combed over today, and he has on another oversized, bright yellow, short-sleeve button-up shirt. He always looks as though he's headed for a luau. He definitely isn't going to find any of those in Wyoming. Maybe it's that damn coconut candle playing tricks on his mind. I swear he buys them in bulk.

"Good evening, Mr. Chu," I greet him with the same polite tone as always. "Another gorgeous summer night, isn't it?"

"Miss Sky, you no pay this week's rent again." His familiar beady eyes ignore my question and flash to the opposite corner of the room. My red backpack sits propped up with clothes sticking out the top as though someone didn't take the time to care. Which, clearly, they didn't. "You no pay, you no sleep here."

"Just a couple more days, I promise. I'm working on finding a new job." It's the truth. After another night at the diner where no one wanted to sit in my section and five tables requested a different waitress, I finally came to the conclusion I need a new job.

I've avoided going to the Black Alcove Bar, where a friend told me I should apply if I want more money. I have no bartending skills. In fact, I don't have many skills for a lot of things. Money does that to a person. Being catered to my entire life has done me no favors for my current situation, but the fact I could be going without another dinner tonight is almost enough to make me suck it up and apply.

"No," he says, a fast answer and solid reminder that no one is catering to me anymore.

"You can't seriously kick me out again." I march toward my bag, swinging it over my shoulder and looping each arm through a strap. Just like my polite tone, this conversation is becoming routine for us. Every other week I can make rent; the other weeks I can't and am out on my ass.

"Find another place to sleep, Miss Sky." You'd think by now he would have compassion for a twenty-two-year-old woman with no place to go. "You bring me money and I let you come back."

"Yeah, yeah, I know."

Another sleepless night in the park won't kill me.

I step back out into the evening sun and head for the gym. Thank god I can manage to keep up on my monthly membership there. The locker I use is the perfect size for my backpack, and they have showers stocked with shampoo, conditioner, and body wash for their members. I can use as many towels I want, and they have hair dryers by every sink. It's not a lot, but it saves me money in that area. I only have to buy makeup or clothes if I need new ones. I've mastered the "I'm your guest and forgot my toothbrush and toothpaste" enough times at the fancier hotels that I'm stocked up for a few months. The only thing I need now is for the gym to offer me a place to sleep and to never raise their rate over forty bucks a month.

Forty bucks I might not be able to afford either if I don't find a new job.

If I get this job at the BA, as everyone has nicknamed it, it better earn me the money I need to get my own place soon. There's no way I can survive overnighters in the park when winter comes around, and being as it's the last week of August, I'm pretty sure winter is going to sneak up on me. I sure don't want to be sleeping at motel Chu forever either, but until I decide what I'm doing with my life, this *is* my life. The only thing I know for sure is that I will never go back to what I should be calling home. It was more like a prison.

"Hey, girl, you need a ride?"

Beth Moyer, the first local to claim me as her friend, slows to a stop in her Nitro. Her red hair waves out the window with the light breeze. Being friends with someone who grew up here and knows everyone has drawn some unwanted attention to me. Sooner or later, people are going to pick up on the fact that I don't have a home. I'd like to resolve that part of my life before they have the time to find out. It still shocks me that I've made it three months, but I also have a feeling it's all about to blow up and everyone is going to know. They would all rush to help me, and that isn't a bad thing, but I don't think I could handle it. I don't want to be pitied.

"No thanks, I'm just headed to the gym," I answer.

Becoming friends with Beth and Alex, whose boyfriend told me to stop into the BA for a job after I admitted to working at the town diner, has made me feel more at home here where I have no home than back in Seattle where I have a family who thinks zeros in a bank account make you better than everyone else. Still, I can't take advantage of my new friends and let them drive me around. That's the whole point of being here. To learn to take care of myself and find out who I am in the process—that's the short version. I made a list and everything.

"Ugh, no wonder you're so skinny. You walk everywhere."

Skinny? Shoot. I have no bed and no food tonight. *Thanks for reminding me, Beth.*

"Yeah, don't tell anyone my secret," I say, winking and continuing on my way.

"Okay, fine, I won't give you a ride, but when are you going to come into the BA for a job? Conner told you to come in like *for-ev-er* ago."

"I was thinking tomorrow."

I keep walking and her car continues to creep along next to me. It would probably make the most sense to just take her up on her offer, but come on—since when in the last few months or even year did I choose the easy route? Nope, I have to make life as complicated as can be.

"Finally!" she cheers out the window, removing her hands from the wheel to clap.

A horn honks, and I trip myself as I jump from the noise.

"Jackass!" Beth hollers behind her. "I'll see you there!" she shouts to me and then flashes a grin before driving off. Her middle finger also went up between her seats for the guy behind her.

Beth doesn't waste time getting to the point in any topic. She knows everyone in this town, and she is always willing to help out any way she can. As many times as I've seen her volunteer to help someone, she can't make any time for herself. If I could give her advice on anything in life without a ton of follow-up questions, it would be that you need to take care of yourself first. If you don't, you'll end up like me, and this isn't the life I'd wish upon anyone.

I reach the gym, other members entering and exiting through the sliding doors. Some have eager faces ready for a workout, and some look ready for a nap. The only actual workout I've done here is yoga, where I met both Alex and Beth. That's a class that will put you to sleep when it's over, for sure.

"Skylar!"

I twist to see who has called my name. Alex. Her blonde hair shines against the sun, and she has a smile on, like always. Jake, her boyfriend's son, is next to her with a basketball tucked under his arm.

"What are you two up to today?" I ask, mainly directing the question toward Jake.

"Alex is gonna shoot some ball with me," he answers, switching the ball to rest under his other arm.

"That sounds fun."

"Do you want to join us?" Alex offers. I walk next to her and Jake as we head inside.

"Oh, no thank you, I have some things I have to do before it gets dark."

"All right, well, I bet we'll be here for a couple hours if you change your mind," she says over her shoulder, as she has to speed up her steps to follow Jake down the hall toward the basketball court.

Once I step into the locker room and adjust to the overwhelming smell of eucalyptus, I stash my bag in my locker and change into the only pair of sweat pants I packed in my dash to get out of my parents' home before they could see me and change my mind. Then again, I most likely could have walked right by them and they wouldn't have noticed.

I grab my hoodie and the list of goals I made when I left, lock up, and leave the gym. I'll add *stop being homeless* to the list as soon as I find a pen.

I head to the coffee shop across from the town park where I read every section of the newspaper until they close at eleven, like I always do on the nights I have to sleep outside. After they close, I find the same tree next to the same bench and I sit back against the bark. *How did I let myself get here?*

I never let myself think for too long on whether I would prefer to be married into a family for money—which is exactly where my life was headed before I left—or out here alone, creating my own way. I could be in Washington right now, sitting on Mack's brown leather couch, snuggled under his arms as we watch a Nicholas Sparks movie … no wait … that's right … I'd be in the kitchen making dinner and cleaning his house like the good little wife he was trying turn me into while he sat in his office making a list of ways for me to present our relationship better to the public eye. That memory alone makes it easier to decide that, homeless or not, this is where I'd rather be. Being me and only me instead of the girl everyone thinks I should be.

Keep reading Just One Moment today !

Don't want to miss out on any new releases from Jami? Subscribe to her mailing list for exclusive bonus epilogues and all the book news!

MORE BOOKS BY JAMI ROGERS

The Black Alcove Series

Just One Kiss

Just One Night

Just One Touch

Just One Moment

Just One Spark

Just One Love

The Kiss Me Crazy Series

Kiss Me Crazy

Love is Crazy

I Want Crazy

The Evergreen Brothers Series

A Boyfriend by Christmas

The Summer Wedding Hoax

A Match by Christmas

The Lust or Bust Series

The Write One

Write About You

The Write Choice

Write That Down

More Than Write

Always Been Write

Standalone Novels

Love Money

Date in the Dark (A New Years Eve Novella)

ACKNOWLEDGMENTS

This story was my hardest to write and also my favorite. I faced the most challenges ever with this story, but once I changed the plot for the third time, I knew I found Conner and Alexis's story, and from there I was swept away. I have a pretty good feeling my family and friends were just as happy as I was when that final draft was finished.

Most of you may notice that I include the same group of people in this section. I'd like to include others and hope to one day do so, but for now, this is my team. These are the people who want to help me be better in any way they can. These people are important to me, each in their own way, and will always remain that way.

Dad, Mom, and Holly—it feels amazing to know that no matter what, you support me and believe in me. Thank you.

Dana Volney—you are mentioned in ALL of my books, and I hope you know how thankful I am for everything you've done for me. You are always there for me and none of this would be as fun and exciting without you.

Kate Maxwell, Megan Phillips, Mallori Roth, and Mom— you are the best Beta readers and you rock. I love how each of you view my stories differently. You all help me succeed in different ways, and I will never be able to thank you enough.

Julie Sturgeon—you sent a pin out that read "I survived

Julie's edits," but I want you to know that your edits are easy to survive because you are thorough and it's easy to see that you want the authors you work with to succeed. You make my novels stronger, and I will gladly take your edits anytime if it means we can continue working together. Thank you!

Trisha Butcher and Alyssa Navarro—thank you for reminding me that I can be both a committed writer and have a social life at the same time. Also, thank you for allowing me to talk about and fill you in on my writing when you do finally get me out of the house. Baby steps

Grant—thank you for putting up with me. I may not always show it, but I appreciate everything you do. Without you being here, I wouldn't be where I am today.

And finally, thank you to the readers, bloggers, and social media fans who are reading the Black Alcove series and spreading the word. Everything you do to support me and my dream is amazing!

ABOUT THE AUTHOR

My name is Jami Rogers and I write new adult contemporary and adult contemporary romance novels. I *love* love and want to share my passion for happily ever afters with the world.

I was born in Wyoming and still live in the cowboy state with my husband, daughter, and two dogs. I like to read, write, run, watch movies/TV and spend time with my family. I'm horrible at returning phone calls and prefer to text, but still struggle to hit the little blue arrow to send a message once I'm finished typing my reply. My husband does 90% of the cooking in our house. Not because I'm busy – I'm just simply a bad cook.

Keep up with Jami by visiting her website www.
authorjamirogers.com
or
Subscribe to her mailing list for exclusive bonus epilogues
and all the book news!